PUCK ME

A WHY CHOOSE HOCKEY ROMANCE

CHARLOTTE BYRD

CHARLOTTE BYRD

dangerously addictive

PRAISE FOR CHARLOTTE BYRD

"Twisted, gripping story full of heat, tension and action. Once again we are caught up in this phenomenal , dark passionate love story that is full of mystery, secrets, suspense and intrigue that continues to keep you on edge!" (Goodreads)

"Must read!" (Goodreads)

"Charlotte will keep you in suspense!" (Goodreads)

"Twisted love story full of power and control!" (Goodreads)

"Just WOW...no one can weave a story quite like Charlotte. This series has me enthralled, with such great story lines and characters." (Goodreads)

"Charlotte Byrd is one of the best authors I have had the pleasure of reading, she spins her storylines around believable characters, and keeps you on the edge of your seat. Five star rating does not do this book/series justice." (Goodreads)

"Suspenseful romance!" (Goodreads)

"Amazing. Scintillating. Drama times 10. Love and heartbreak. They say what you don't know can't hurt you, but that's not true in this book." (Goodreads)

"I loved this book, it is fast paced on the crime plot, and super-hot on the drama, I would say the perfect mix. This suspense will have your heart racing and your blood pumping. I am happy to recommend this thrilling and exciting book, that I just could not stop reading once I started. This story will keep you glued to the pages and you will find yourself cheering this couple on to finding their happiness. This book is filled with energy, intensity and heat. I loved this book so much. It was super easy to get swept up into and once there, I was very happy to stay." (*Goodreads*)

"BEST AUTHOR YET! Charlotte has done it again! There is a reason she is an amazing author and she continues to prove it! I was definitely not disappointed in this series!!" (*Goodreads*)

"LOVE!!! I loved this book and the whole series!!! I just wish it didn't have to end. I am definitely a fan for life!!! (*Goodreads*)

"Extremely captivating, sexy, steamy, intriguing, and intense!" (*Goodreads*) ⭐⭐⭐⭐⭐

"Addictive and impossible to put down." (*Goodreads*) ⭐⭐⭐⭐⭐

"What a magnificent story from the 1st book through book 6 it never slowed down always surprising the reader in one way or the other. Nicholas and Olive's paths crossed in a most unorthodox way and that's how their story begins it's exhilarating with that nail biting suspense that keeps you riding on the edge the whole series. You'll love it!" (*Goodreads*) ⭐⭐⭐⭐⭐

"What is Love Worth. This is a great epic ending to this series. Nicholas and Olive have a deep connection and the mystery surrounding the deaths of the people he is accused of murdering is to be read. Olive is one strong woman with deep convictions. The twists, angst, confusion is all put together to make this worthwhile read." (*Goodreads*) ⭐⭐⭐⭐⭐

"Fast-paced romantic suspense filled with twists and turns, danger, betrayal, and so much more." (*Goodreads*) ⭐⭐⭐⭐⭐

"Decadent, delicious, & dangerously addictive!" (*Goodreads*) ⭐⭐⭐⭐⭐

"Titillation so masterfully woven, no reader can resist its pull. A MUST-BUY!" (*Goodreads*) ⭐⭐⭐⭐⭐

"Captivating!" (*Goodreads*) ⭐⭐⭐⭐⭐

"Sexy, secretive, pulsating chemistry…" (*Goodreads*) ⭐⭐⭐⭐⭐

"Charlotte Byrd is a brilliant writer. I've read loads and I've laughed and cried. She writes a balanced book with brilliant characters. Well done!" (*Goodreads*) ⭐⭐⭐⭐⭐

"Hot, steamy, and a great storyline." (*Goodreads*) ⭐⭐⭐⭐⭐

"My oh my….Charlotte has made me a fan for life." (*Goodreads*) ⭐⭐⭐⭐⭐

"Wow. Just wow. Charlotte Byrd leaves me speechless and humble… It definitely kept me on the edge of my seat. Once you pick it up, you won't put it down." (*Goodreads*) ⭐⭐⭐⭐⭐

" Intrigue, lust, and great characters...what more could you ask for?!" (*Goodreads*)

WANT TO BE THE FIRST TO KNOW ABOUT MY UPCOMING SALES, NEW RELEASES AND EXCLUSIVE GIVEAWAYS?

Sign up for my newsletter and get a FREE book: https://dl.bookfunnel.com/gp3o8yvmxd

Join my Facebook Group: https://www.facebook.com/groups/276340079439433/

Bonus Points: Follow me on BookBub and Goodreads!

ABOUT CHARLOTTE BYRD

Charlotte Byrd is the bestselling author of romantic suspense novels. She has sold over 1.5 Million books and has been translated into five languages.

She lives near Palm Springs, California with her husband, son, a toy Australian Shepherd and a Ragdoll cat. Charlotte is addicted to books and Netflix and she loves hot weather and crystal blue water.

Write her here:

charlotte@charlotte-byrd.com

Check out her books here:

www.charlotte-byrd.com

Connect with her here:

www.tiktok.com/charlottebyrdbooks

www.facebook.com/charlottebyrdbooks

www.instagram.com/charlottebyrdbooks

Sign up for my newsletter: https://www.
subscribepage.com/byrdVIPList

Join my Facebook Group: https://www.facebook.
com/groups/276340079439433/

Bonus Points: Follow me on BookBub and
Goodreads!

[a] amazon.com/Charlotte-Byrd/e/B013MN45Q6

[f] facebook.com/charlottebyrdbooks

[d] tiktok.com/charlottebyrdbooks

[BB] bookbub.com/profile/charlotte-byrd

[O] instagram.com/charlottebyrdbooks

[X] x.com/byrdauthor

ALSO BY CHARLOTTE BYRD

All books are available at ALL major retailers! If you can't find it, please email me at charlotte@ charlotte-byrd.com

Somerset Harbor
Hate Mate (Cargill Brothers 1)
Best Laid Plans (Cargill Brothers 2)
Picture Perfect (Cargill Brothers 3)
Always Never (Cargill Brothers 4)
Kiss Me Again (Macmillan Brothers 1)
Say You'll Stay (Macmillan Brothers 2)
Never Let Go (Macmillan Brothers 3)
Keep Me Close (Macmillan Brothers 4)

Hockey Why Choose
One Pucking Night (Novella)
Kiss and Puck

Pucking Disaster

Puck Me

Puck It

Tell me Series

Tell Me to Stop

Tell Me to Go

Tell Me to Stay

Tell Me to Run

Tell Me to Fight

Tell Me to Lie

Tell Me to Stop Box Set Books 1-6

Black Series

Black Edge

Black Rules

Black Bounds

Black Contract

Black Limit

Black Edge Box Set Books 1-5

Dark Intentions Series

Dark Intentions

Dark Redemption

Dark Sins

Dark Temptations

Dark Inheritance

Dark Intentions Box Set Books 1-5

Tangled Series
Tangled up in Ice
Tangled up in Pain
Tangled up in Lace
Tangled up in Hate
Tangled up in Love

Tangled up in Ice Box Set Books 1-5

The Perfect Stranger Series
The Perfect Stranger
The Perfect Cover
The Perfect Lie
The Perfect Life
The Perfect Getaway

The Perfect Stranger Box Set Books 1-5

Wedlocked Trilogy
Dangerous Engagement
Lethal Wedding
Fatal Wedding

Dangerous Engagement Box Set Books 1-3

Lavish Trilogy
Lavish Lies

Lavish Betrayal
Lavish Obsession

Lavish Lies Box Set Books 1-3

All the Lies Series
All the Lies
All the Secrets
All the Doubts

All the Lies Box Set Books 1-3

Not into you Duet
Not into you
Still not into you

Standalone Novels
Dressing Mr. Dalton
Debt
Offer
Unknown

ABOUT PUCK ME

A secret relationship with three professional hockey players who aren't exactly great at sharing the same woman is a difficult thing to balance...

Ash and Soren are about to leave for Seattle and the four of us need sometime to connect. They surprise me with a lake house rental where we can drink wine, have lots of steamy nights and fall even more in love with each other.

When they leave, our foursome is torn apart and Ryder and I are just not the same. But when we start to spend more and more time together, we realize just how much we are falling for one another.

Keeping this why choose relationship a secret has been a challenge, and I'm tested when my friend Corey finds out that I am finally seeing someone.

Given that I'm the team's psychologist, no one can ever know that I'm dating three pro hockey players at once and we're in love…but all of that is about to change.

What happens when we get close to being exposed? What happens when our love is tested?

tropes:

- hockey romance
- why choose
- MFM
- new adult
- angsty/steamy
- workplace romance

1

HARLOW

I can think of worse ways to spend a long weekend than lying out by a lake, sunning myself under a cloudless sky.

"I'm going to grab another six pack from the fridge." Ryder gets up from the blanket spread out on the dock and stretches. I won't bother pretending not to ogle his sun-kissed body. He's a thing of beauty, and I'd be stupid not to appreciate what's in front of me. Especially when there's nobody around who'd care. The freedom of being able to show affection—and yeah, flat-out lust—in public is intoxicating.

"Take it easy on that," I warn him, lifting my sunglasses to give him a serious stare. "If we're going water skiing later, it's not a good idea to drink too much."

"One six-pack for the four of us isn't going to do any harm." He turns toward the cabin we've rented for the weekend, then chuckles before he's taken a step. "Looks like I'm not the only one with that idea."

I turn my head to find Ash and Soren coming our way, both of them dressed in swim trunks the way Ryder is. "Thought we could use a little refreshment," Soren calls out, raising the beer above his head.

"Careful. Mom doesn't think it's a good idea for us to do too much drinking before we get out on the water." Ryder pretends not to notice my scowl.

"Ooh. I didn't know caring about your safety was such a bummer. Remind me not to care."

"She's probably right." That doesn't stop Soren from tossing a can of beer Ryder's way. "And that's why we're not going to overdo it."

"I can't believe I've never been here before." Ash settles in on my towel and sits with his arms draped over his knees. "I've seen it on TV, but never in person. This is gorgeous."

It really is. The lake mirrors the blue sky and sparkles in the midday sunshine. A soft breeze ripples the water and cools my skin.

And I'm surrounded by hot hockey players. Life has been worse, for sure.

"I don't know. I've had my eye on other scenery." Soren winks at me before taking a long gulp from his can.

"You never waste an opportunity, do you," Ryder grumbles, but I know he's only joking. At least, I hope so.

This is still so new. It's unfamiliar territory for all four of us. I know it's not going to be perfect, but there will be times when there's strain and sore feelings. No matter how the three of them swear up and down that they're good with the way things are, I'm not naïve. There will be bumps in the road.

But right now, everything seems like smooth sailing. I'm sure part of that has to do with knowing half of our little foursome will be up in Seattle for an undetermined amount of time.

Ryder took it well, finding out he wouldn't be receiving a two-way contract to play with the Orcas. "Don't worry. I'll stay here and keep her safe." Sure, he joked about it, but I sensed the disappointment under his grin. Even though I had nothing to do with who got chosen, I wanted to apologize. I wanted to hold him and tell him it's okay, that he'll get his chance.

But I can't show favoritism, right? I don't want to start trouble. I wonder if it'll ever get easier, this feeling that I have to carefully consider everything I say and do.

This will be our last time together for a while, and we all want to make the most of it. And we have since our arrival yesterday. Let's just say it's a miracle I can walk, after the hours we spent exploring the cabin and each other.

It's so easy to feel lighthearted and happy out here, watching the sail boats and jet skis crisscrossing the lake. There's happy laughter ringing out across the water, and it makes me smile. I needed this. An escape. I don't have to look over my shoulder or watch what I say in front of Coach Kozak. It wasn't until we got out here that I understood how stressful it is, working hard to make sure we're all safe in this relationship.

Especially me. Let's face it, they would keep their jobs if anybody found out they were sleeping with the team's therapist. Me? I don't even want to think about what would happen to my career. I've done enough thinking about it, anyway. Obsessing, worrying.

And yet I'm still with them, because there's no place else I'd rather be. I could never have imagined my life turning out this way. I guess that's sort of the point, really. We can't predict. We can only do our best with what life gives us.

Right now, life is giving me the opportunity to do nothing but have fun and drink and have incredible sex. I'm not about to start complaining.

———

"YOU REALLY SHOULD GET out on the water." Ryder flips back his hair, now wet thanks to the way he wiped out on his skis. He was doing well for a while there – much better than I would have.

Which is exactly why I shake my head. "No, thank you. You know I'm not athletic. It's fun being on the boat and watching you guys." Even if my heart practically stopped beating when he hit the water with a crash that sounded much worse than it actually was.

"You'll love it. And you won't get hurt."

"So you say. Something tells me I'll find a way."

The boat's pilot speeds up once Ash is ready, and a rush of adrenaline slams into me when I watch him gracefully handle the boat's wake. He does much better than Ryder and even Soren, who up until now managed the most impressive run. Ash leaves him in the dust, bending his body this way and that and

CHARLOTTE BYRD

even using one hand at times, switching back-and-forth depending on the direction he's leaning.

"You fucking show off!" Soren calls out with his hands cupped around his mouth.

"He's a ringer," Ryder grumbles, shaking his head. "And there he was, acting like he'd never done this before."

All I can do is laugh at their outrage. I love their competitive nature—at least, when they're not competing over me. Water skiing seems like a much safer competition. I don't feel like I'm stuck in the middle.

By the time we're ready to head back to the cabin for something to eat and maybe a little rest, my skin is sun-bronzed and I'm happily tired out. I can't keep from smiling as I trudge across the dock, then up to the cabin, while the guys good-naturedly bicker over their performance.

"What can I say? I'm just better at it than you are."

"That was not your first time, and don't bother pretending it was." Soren shakes his head and clicks his tongue like he's disappointed.

"You've seen me surf, dick. It's not that different. Hell, I had something to hold onto. That's a step up from what we're used to."

"I won't be satisfied until we get this one on the water." I glance behind me in time to find Ryder jerking his chin in my direction.

"I'm sorry. Does *this one* not have a name anymore?"

"To tell you the truth, there are other sports I want to watch her perform." Soren's wink leaves me blushing, or maybe that's just the flush on my cheeks after a day spent in the sun.

"Gee. I wonder what you could be talking about." To tell the truth, I'm only playing around, pretending to be insulted.

"Now that you mention it, I wouldn't mind that, myself." Ash falls in step beside me and gives me a wicked little smile.

"I am so shocked," I retort. "Usually, you're not a complete horn dog at all."

"You mean you could watch me out there, flying over the water like a god, and you don't want to jump on this?" He spreads his arms wide, looking down at his bare chest. It's impressive, I won't pretend otherwise, but for the sake of the joke I merely shrug.

"Like you said, you're used to it from surfing. I'm not nearly as impressed anymore." When his face falls, I have to laugh. "What? You can dish it out, but you can't take it."

"I think that's the most accurate way you could ever sum him up," Soren points out with a laugh as we climb the steps onto the open porch in front of the cabin. There's a refreshing breeze coming off the water that stirs the hair at the nape of my neck. I can't wait to sit out here later, as the sun goes down and the air turns cooler. It's really like being in another world, and I want to soak in every second of it while I can.

I want to soak in every second with them.

A wave of longing almost takes me out at the knees, but I push past it, forcing a smile I no longer feel. I'm going to miss them. I'm going to miss this. No, it won't be forever, and it might make things easier with two of the three out of town. Less of a chance of getting caught, all that.

But I'm sort of starting to depend on them. They've become part of my life that I'm not looking forward to giving up even for a short amount of time.

I might even be falling for them.

2

ASH

"Are you going to miss this?"

I look over at Soren, both of us lounging back in a pair of leather recliners while we wait for Ryder to grab snacks from the kitchen. Harlow requested a little time to herself so she can read on the porch and chat with her friend Ruby, who is apparently having guy drama. Our game is currently paused, and we're taking a much-needed breather after more than an hour of combat. It's a different way of letting off steam — we can't spend all day taking turns on Harlow, after all.

"This place? Sure. It's great."

"You know that's not what I mean. While we're gone. Do you think you'll miss... this?"

"Will you?" God, I hate the way he lifts an eyebrow like he knows something I'm not willing to admit. It's beyond irritating, sometimes, knowing that he knows me. There's only so much I can get away with being vague about.

"What do you want me to say? Do you want me to tell you I'll cry myself to sleep every night?"

"It's a little closer to sincerity, at least."

"What about you? Will you miss this?"

"Of course, I will. See?" he asks with a smirk. "It's easy to admit you have feelings. At least, it's easy when you're not afraid to talk about them."

"Who said I was afraid? Maybe I'm just not as, you know, in touch with my emotions, or whatever."

"Whoever was in charge of snacks really did a good job." Ryder pauses on his way into the open, airy living room area. "Oh, wait. That was me."

He sits down between us in a third chair facing the enormous flatscreen TV bolted to the wood paneled wall. I reach over to grab a handful of chips and a soda while Soren does the same. I'd love to spend the afternoon with a cold beer, but whiskey dick is a very real thing and considering this is our last opportunity to be with Harlow for a while, I want to make sure I'm not screwing myself over later on.

Will I miss this? What a thing to ask. Obviously, I'm going to miss this. I'll miss her. The thread that connects us more thoroughly than hockey ever has. I don't want to imagine how much it will suck to be apart – especially when nobody knows how long it'll be before we're together again.

Isn't this a bitch? I'm getting what I wanted. This is my chance to show what I can really do. A shot at the big leagues. The opportunity to impress the right people, to make a lasting impression. This is what it's all been for. All the training, all the work, the sacrifices over the years. It's all for this.

I didn't expect to feel this… torn.

It's a little weird around Ryder right now, too. He's been cool with the way things panned out. Cooler than I expected, even. He's not exactly a guy who hides his feelings, let's just put it that way. My heart sank a little when I found out he wouldn't be coming along with us. He wants it, too – he wants it bad. And he's come a long way, refining that raw talent he was apparently born with. It would be one thing seeing him in the locker room, training with him, all that, but this prolonged proximity adds another layer to the situation. I feel like I have to watch what I say around him, and I can tell Soren feels the same. He always gets this pinched, almost constipated look on his face whenever we talk about work.

He likes to act like he's always easy-going, unaffected by feelings, shit like that. Maybe I know him better than he knows himself. He doesn't want to rub it in Ryder's face or anything, and even though I know a lot of it has to do with keeping our relationship with Harlow steady and drama free, he doesn't want to make things any worse for the guy. After all, we were already friends before we got together with Harlow. All the jealousy and tension from the early days aside, I would like to keep it that way. I know Soren would, too.

Obviously, I'm not the only one thinking along these lines even after we get the game started again. "I don't think I'm ready to go back tomorrow," Ryder muses.

It's a funny thing about video games like this. When you're playing, it somehow makes it easier to open up and say the things you wouldn't normally say if you were looking somebody in the face. With all of us focused on the screen, it's easier to say what's on our minds.

"I know," Soren agrees. "It's been pretty sweet, being out here. Not having to hide anything from anybody."

"And that's easier for her, too," I add. It seems sort of funny talking about her while I'm blowing the heads off some fake enemies on the screen.

"I guess I'll have to keep an eye on her while you guys are gone." Ryder's voice is even, maybe a little too much. Like he's pretending to be lighthearted and joking about it when underneath there's something deeper.

"So long as you keep your eye on her and your hands off her," Soren warns. He, too, wants to make it sound like he's joking when I don't think he is.

"Let's not even go there," I decide. "We all know the rules. It'll be fine."

"It's not myself I'm worried about." Ryder looks my way, then at Soren. "I'm more worried about you guys."

"I'm sure it'll be fine."

"Yeah," Soren agrees with me. "I don't think a couple of weeks is too much time to go without getting laid. Fuck, did I actually say that?"

"That's not what I meant." Ryder expertly fights his way out of an ambush situation, blowing the heads off a bunch of shuffling zombies. "I was talking about the temptation you'll come up against out there."

"What temptation?" I shouldn't scoff, but I have to. "I never even thought about that."

"It's going to be all around you when you're out there. I mean, we all know how it is already. Go to the bar after a game and there are going to be plenty of girls there who recognize a bunch of jocks when they see them, even if they don't know the names or the faces."

"That's true," Soren muses. "It's like they've got a sixth sense."

"Go out after the game with some of the guys up there and see how much worse it'll get – or better, depending on how you look at it."

"Stop trying to put shit in our heads," I grumble. "It's not going to work."

"Work? Who said anything about me putting shit in your heads?" he asks, all innocent. "I'm just trying to make a point."

"Well, you don't need to," I retort. "We're not going to be tempted."

"I sure as hell hope not, because if you fuck this up, I might have to kill you." Like he's trying to prove his point, he fires a few rounds in the game.

I see his point, and how he has a stake in things. I mean, when we made our arrangement, it was the four of us together. There's no excuse for sneaking off without the three of us guys being present all at once. It's the three of us with her, or it's none of us.

Meaning, if one of us drops out, it could be the end of everything.

It's a lot to ask, but Harlow's worth it. I would rather share her than never be with her at all. And that's more than enough to make me keep my hands to myself while I'm away. I'm not trying to ruin a good thing for the sake of getting my dick wet with some random stranger.

"So long as you're not tempted," I counter. "No screwing around."

"I know the rules." That's all he'll say, but then it's all he needs to say. We all understand each other.

Though there's something else. Something I wouldn't dare say out loud. Hell, it's something I can hardly admit to myself.

I don't want anybody else. I only want her, because I'm pretty sure I'm falling for her. Hard.

It might be the worst idea ever, but there's no helping it. I'm not even sure I want to.

3

RYDER

The energy in the master bedroom is almost electric as the three of us wait for Harlow to join us. One last night, and then who knows the next time we'll all be together.

I'm not exactly good in situations like this. Wondering, not knowing for sure what's going to happen. How long it's going to take before the guys return. I guess it has to do with the uncertainty I faced throughout my childhood — ironically, I could work it out with the team therapist, but that would mean confessing to Harlow that I'm a little antsy. I'll be vulnerable in front of her, but that's a little too much to ask.

I hate not being able to predict what's going to happen. I hate that there's a question mark hanging in the air even now, while we wait, none of us looking at each other. Without Harlow in the room to draw our attention, there's nowhere to look but at the walls, the floor, the ceiling, even. The room is big enough that we have space to pace around a little, impatient. She already lit a bunch of candles, and there's a definite romantic sort of glow, but without her, it's sort of awkward.

Luckily, she doesn't keep us waiting for long. All three of us go still the second the door opens. In the light from the hallway, she might as well be an angel, wrapped in a white satin robe with her blonde waves framing her shoulders.

She takes my breath away. That's the only way to describe the effect she has on me the moment I set eyes on her. It's like a weakness that comes over me all at once. I'm frozen to the spot and at the same time, fighting to keep from going to her, wrapping her in my arms, and claiming her all for myself.

Without saying a word, she steps into the room, her bare feet silent against the wood planks. As she moves, she slowly tugs the belt holding her robe closed, so by the time she reaches the king size bed it hangs open to reveal glimpses of bare skin. She's naked.

The robe falls from her shoulders, and I'm not the only one ogling her, drinking in the sight of every curve, admiring the way the candlelight plays off her full ass and hips, the way her tits sway gently as she climbs onto the bed and faces us on her knees. We move slowly, inching toward her, and I'm not the only one who's already sporting a raging hard-on. She has us all under her spell.

"This is our last night together for a while," she explains in a throaty murmur. "I didn't want to waste any time."

Neither do I. Especially since I have to go without touching, tasting, feeling for an unknown amount of time. At least those two get to go to Seattle and play for the Orcas. At least they have something to show for it. Sure, I'll have her to myself, but I already know the struggle of fighting my need for her. It's not exactly fun, and I wouldn't wish it on anyone.

She holds out her arms, beckoning silently, and I slide out of my shorts before being the first to climb onto the bed with her. I can't help it — my arms slide around her body and I pull her close, groaning when my swollen head brushes her flat stomach before I sink my hands into her hair and draw her in for a deep kiss. I need to have something to remember, don't I? Her helpless moans once I've plunged my tongue deep into her mouth are a good start.

"Don't be greedy." As usual, Soren has a hint of laughter in his voice as he takes Harlow's jaw in his hands and turns her head to the side so he can be the one tasting her full lips, while I caress her supple ass. The hunger she stirs to life without trying is endless, bottomless. I could spend the next year of my life doing nothing but this and it still wouldn't be enough.

Ash takes his place behind her and it's a little awkward, having to move my hands so I'm not touching him instead of her. For one wild moment, I see myself throwing them out of the room and locking the door, forcing them to listen, while I take her mercilessly. Loud, rough, so hard she'd scream my name while they would pound on the door. It's a nice little fantasy.

But she would never go for that, which is all that stops me. Instead, I dip my hand between her thighs and stroke her bald lips, already slick with her hot juices. Her head falls back against Ash's shoulder, her tongue still tangled with Soren's. I lower my head to take one of her pretty, pink nipples in my mouth.

"Just like that..." she moans. I'm greedy for the sound of her pleasure and the satisfaction of knowing I'm the one giving it to her. That greed drives me to slide two fingers inside her slick, tight tunnel and pump them slowly while thumbing her clit.

Ash and Soren take turns kissing her, while the other laps at her throat and they both stroke every bare patch of skin they can find. Though it's my hair her hands run through, it's me she's moaning for the loudest. I am the one massaging her G-spot and stroking her pink nub, working her body, claiming her first orgasm tonight. I don't even care that my dick is aching, already dripping precum by the time she begins tightening around my digits. "Yes, Harlow. Come for me, baby."

Suddenly she does, arching her back and going rigid for a heartbeat before shuddering. Her juices coat my knuckles by the time she's finished with my fingers still inside her, moving slowly, almost lazily to draw out her pleasure.

Once it's over she goes limp and sags against Ash, who gets out of the way so she can lie back. Her eyes open in time to watch me lick her nectar from my hand. The sight makes her gasp softly, but she smiles. She likes it.

How did I ever find this perfect woman? I'm starting to think I don't deserve her. None of us do.

Ash parts her legs, burying his head between them and licking up what's left of what I drew from her. She reaches out blindly and takes hold of Soren's dick, stroking it as she moans for Ash. For a minute or two, it's enough just to watch, stroking myself to the sight of her being pleasured. When Soren drives himself into her mouth, she takes him almost greedily. Even if it's not me working her body, seeing her lost in pleasure is the next best thing. And she is lost, writhing and moaning, grinding against Ash's face.

Soren groans, disappointed, when she releases him with a popping sound and looks around. "Ryder," she whispers, reaching for me with the hand whose nails were raking over Ash's back seconds ago. Nothing can stop me from obeying her command, and soon she's stroking me while sucking Soren like her life depends on it.

Her timing couldn't be better, since she takes me into her mouth only seconds before her hips lift and her lusty moans rise in pitch, turning to something closer to desperate squeals.

Instead of letting her up for air, I take the back of her head in my hand and hold her in place, pumping my hips, fucking her face while she builds into another orgasm. The vibrations from her throat run through me – it's a delicious thrill, but I have to fight it off. Not yet. I can't come yet. There's so much more to do to her tonight.

Finally, I take mercy and let her go in time for her to gulp air between cries of bliss.

"You're so pretty when you come." Soren plays with her, stroking her stomach, her tits, while she strokes him in the aftermath.

Her smile is knowing, pleased. "You guys are so good at making me come."

"How about you get on your knees like a good girl so I can do that for you?" All three of us back off, while she rolls onto her stomach, then up onto her hands and knees for Soren to take her from behind. I get a glimpse of her glistening pussy the instant before he enters her and admire the way it pulses in the aftershocks. I'm not sure if she's finished coming yet before he begins fucking her in deep, sure strokes.

"Greedy," he gasps through gritted teeth. "So greedy for my cock. trying to milk me dry already."

"Yes… Yes…" She thrusts against him, and it might be the hottest thing I've ever seen in my life. Watching her take him the way he takes her. I didn't know there were women like her in the real world, outside of fantasies. Somebody so… enthusiastic. Eager. And she's not afraid to ask for what she wants.

Like now, when her head swings from side to side. "Well? Did you guys suddenly lose interest?"

No. I don't think I ever could.

4

SOREN

"I think I could get used to this." I turn away from the bar, leaning against the brass rail with a bottle of beer in one hand. All around me, there are people busy celebrating a win for the Orcas earlier tonight. More than a few of the team's regular players are gathered around us, and with them a ton of fans.

Including more than a few cute girls. Very cute.

"What, being treated like a star?"

I don't like the grim tone in my friend's voice. I turn to Ash, who's sipping his beer with his back to the room. "What's up your ass? You would think we lost tonight."

"No, the game was great."

"Why do you look and sound like you're at a funeral?"

He lifts a shoulder and won't look at me. I think that's what takes my surprised concern and turns it into something sharper. "What's your problem?" I ask before elbowing him in the ribs until he finally glares my way.

"I don't have a problem."

"Then why aren't you acting like you're having fun? That's the whole point, right?"

"What's the whole point?"

"Replacing injured players, showing our stuff. Stepping up from the minors, the way we both wanted. Enjoying the fruits of our labor after a game."

"It's not like it's permanent."

"You don't have to tell me that." I swear, when he decides he's going to be a whiny bitch, he really commits.

The fact is, he's been a whiny bitch the past few days. I think I know why, and I would rather bite off my tongue than say it out loud. He's good. He's very good, probably too good for the minor league.

But this is a whole new world. Same game, but with the intensity turned up tenfold. It's not exactly like we screw around on the ice or anything — it's a game, but we don't treat it like it's fun.

The stakes are so much higher here. There's less room for mistakes.

And back home, we're big fish in a smaller pond. This pond is much larger. More like a lake. There are much bigger fish swimming around.

And he's always taking everything too seriously. Sometimes I wonder how we get along so well, being so different. Sure, I want this to be my full-time life — if not in Seattle, then in another city. But I'm not kidding myself. I'm able to look at this as a fun experience even if it doesn't pan out into something bigger and better.

Which is why I can't for the life of me figure out why he would ruin a good thing by being so damn glum.

"You had a good game."

He rolls his eyes and scoffs loud enough for me to hear even over the almost deafening roar filling the bar. "Do me a favor and don't patronize me, okay? I know I had a good game. That's never been a question."

"Then what is it?"

He opens his mouth. He closes his mouth. Finally, he sighs. "I don't know, man. There's something off with me."

"Don't tell me you're getting sick or something."

"No, nothing like that."

"Hey. For real." I wait for him to look my way before clapping a hand over his shoulder. "You need anything, you know you can talk to me. Right? That's never going to change."

"I know. Thanks." His smile is brief enough that I might have imagined it, and he quickly polishes off his beer. "I think I'm gonna go back to the hotel. I'm not feeling it tonight." He glances around and snickers. "I thought we partied back home."

He's got a good point. The ice isn't the only place where the intensity picks up in this strange new world we've landed in. A few of the guys are currently doing shots to see which of them can drink the most and still be able to walk a straight line. There's a crowd around them, most of them laying bets on who will win. A couple of the players who I happen to know are married have drifted off to dark corners with eager looking girls. There's dancing all around us, the floor is sticky with spilled alcohol, I can barely hear myself think over the laughter, cheering, squealing.

As tired as Ash seems with all of it, the opposite is true for me. I'm buzzing — alive, vibrating with energy. I want to celebrate a win. Who knows if I'll get another chance like this?

Still, I sort of feel like I have to be a decent friend. "Want me to come with you?"

"No way. Have fun." This time, there's no asking myself if I imagined the look that comes over his face. Even in the vaguely purple light coming from the neon signs over the bar, I can read it plain as day. He's concerned. Doubtful.

Suspicious? He should know me better than that. I don't want to call him out on it and start anything, but I can't help wanting to ask him what the hell he's thinking. It's not like I would do anything to jeopardize what we have with Harlow.

Not like there hasn't been plenty of opportunity already.

But I've been a good boy. And I will be now that Ash is leaving, raising his hand to say good night as he exits.

The fact is, I've never been a cheater, but I can understand why some of these guys can't seem to stay faithful. Women find out you're a pro athlete and they make it their mission to hook up with you. They might as well launch themselves out of a cannon. That's how it feels tonight, when everywhere I look, there are wide eyes inviting me. Sexy smiles. Women in short skirts and tight dresses, women with long hair they swing close to your face as they lean in to shout at the bartender, asking for a drink. Women who brush their bodies against mine and offer coy, flirty smiles.

Smiles I can't ignore. I never could. I'm a natural flirt – I always have been, ever since I discovered the difference between boys and girls. I like women, what can I say? I like being around them. And I like it when they like me.

That doesn't mean my feelings for Harlow have changed. Far from it. I miss her like crazy and have used our last night together as jerk-off material in the shower more than once. It's nice to know she's home waiting for me. I can't wait to tell her all about this experience.

But there are certain things I'll leave out. Like how damn difficult it is to turn away from the latest coy, welcoming smile offered by a petite brunette with tits I would've liked to fuck under different circumstances.

"You're one of the Orcas, aren't you?" She practically has to shout to be heard, and even then I need to lean down to hear her better.

"I am." I'm not trying to explain the whole two-way contract situation, and I doubt she'd care, either way. I'm a player right now, and that's what she cares about.

"That is so hot. Hockey players are my favorite." Like she's talking about the food she likes best to eat, or the music she likes to listen to. Out of all sports, hockey players are her favorite. Doesn't matter which one.

"Cool." Do not engage. Do not. It took long enough to get Harlow to a point where we could have a relationship, unusual as it is. I'm not going to screw that up for some girl whose face I won't remember by morning.

No matter how tempting she is when she presses her arms together and practically presents her tits to me. Her deep cleavage is plainly visible thanks to the low-cut tank top tucked into a pair of jeans so tight, they might as well have been painted on her body. My dick twitches, but that's an unconscious reaction. I can't help it.

What I can help is the way my gaze keeps darting down toward her cleavage.

Maybe I should've left with Ash, after all.

And maybe, just maybe, our unusual arrangement isn't the arrangement for me if I'm having such a hard time disassociating from the fun going on all around me. I can see myself living in this world. I can see it all too easily.

But how could I, and still stay faithful to Harlow?

Did I make a mistake committing to her in the first place?

5

HARLOW

"I can't believe how excited I am." I hold up my hands so Corey can see how they're trembling. "You would think I was the one playing today."

"It's cute. You want your team to do well. And they will," she adds with a solemn nod. "How can they not, with you helping them?"

"Be careful. Don't have too much faith in my abilities."

She rolls her eyes and shakes her head. "Sometimes, you're enough to make a saint swear."

"I'm just saying. It's one thing for everybody to do better in scrimmage games and feel more confident and all that." We take our seats in the packed arena, and I rub my hands on the legs of my jeans to wipe away the nervous sweat that coats my palms. "Playing against another team? That's another story."

"Are you worried about the guys making up for Ash and Soren not being here?"

I blow out a long, shaky breath. "It's one thing for a plan to work on paper. Do you know what I mean?"

"Sure." Still, she gives me one of her bright, hopeful smiles. "Maybe don't be too hard on yourself if things are a little bumpy today. It's only the first game."

She's right. I need to chill. After I take a deep breath, I scan the bench and find Coach Kozak talking with a couple of the players. I thought he'd be as nervous as I am and expected his anxiety to get worse as the season opener approached. But no, he has clearly adapted the attitude of a Buddhist monk. What's meant to be will be. I have no idea what led to this new mellow attitude, but whatever it is, I hope he doesn't lose it anytime soon. I only hope it's not all because of the work I did to put together new lines to cover for the team's loss, since I'm still not sure it'll work out.

My loss, too. It hasn't been easy, these days without the two of them driving me crazy. It's weird, not seeing them on the bench. My heart aches a little no matter how hard I try to push the feeling away. This is good for them. For their careers. I can't be selfish and allow my needs to get in the way of that. We had an amazing weekend together, the four of us. I need to cling to those memories.

Especially since Ryder and I are sort of hands-off at the moment. We have to be. That's the agreement we all came to when we started this crazy arrangement. I'm either with all of them at once, or none of them. Sure, we can't avoid each other at work – we even had a session this week, the way I did with several of the other players. He was completely professional the whole time, without so much as a single double entendre or a reference to the time we spent together outside of work.

I'm sure it's totally wrong, but I almost kind of wished he would try to push the envelope a little. What can I say? I'm lonesome and maybe a little bit horny. I would've shot him down, obviously. I don't want to hurt anybody. But it might've been nice to have confirmation that he's still thinking about me even if we've had to put things on pause for now.

My pulse starts racing when the players take the ice, and my eyes are glued to Ryder. What's he thinking? What's he feeling? He doesn't want to admit that it's a little weird, being one of the team's best players, but not being asked to go up to the Orcas even for a little while. I've made a point not to say anything, since I don't want to offend him. He has a lot of pride, after all. It might look like an assumption on my part. Knowing him, he'll be more likely to shut down and retreat inside himself. I don't want that.

Once the puck drops, there's too much going on for me to obsess any longer. The arena is packed and I can't lie, it's exciting to hear the fans cheering and urging the players on. They're the element that's been missing. I can watch all the hours of scrimmage I want – and I have, and then some. But they are the missing piece to the puzzle, the energy that seems to fill the enormous space. I have to imagine the cheering and screaming helps the players, too. They're working at a higher level than I've ever seen them, even during training camp when they were being put through their paces.

And my heart soars when it's clear, Ryder is taking a leadership position in all of this. When he's on the bench, he's bolstering the other players, hyping them up. On the ice, he's like a ghost or something, gliding almost effortlessly, practically flying. "He's incredible!" Corey shouts in the middle of the chaos, and I don't have to ask who she means. Ryder's the clear standout star today. My heart is so full, it might burst.

Especially when he gets an assist on the first goal. "Yes!" I scream before jumping to my feet along with everybody else around us. "Yes, Ryder!" It's silly, but I almost want to tell the people seated around us that I know him personally. I'm just so proud, that's all.

And I'm even prouder when he gets a second assist in the second period. Coach Kozak is beside himself, clapping and shouting, pointing to Ryder as he skates past. "That has to feel good," Corey observes, clapping. Yes, I'm sure it does. For one crazy second, I wish more than ever that I didn't have to hide, that we didn't have to act like there's nothing between us. If I were his girlfriend, I could throw my arms around him after the game and it wouldn't matter who was watching. I could kiss him and tell him how proud I am.

All I can do is play the part of the proud but distant therapist.

"He's really stepped up," I observe as evenly as I can while my heart soars. "I know the coach is thrilled."

"Don't even pretend you have nothing to do with it."

"Okay, maybe I helped a little. He did sort of have a chip on his shoulder when we first met."

"Sometimes the people with the chip on their shoulder are the ones who work the hardest, because they have something to prove." She makes a good point. But I guess she would know, having skated competitively for years. She's gone toe-to-toe with athletes her entire life.

What impresses me the most about him, personal feelings aside, is that he doesn't try to be the star. He's not the one scoring the goals. It's enough for him to pass the puck and let somebody else get the glory. He's come such a long way. I would love nothing more than to talk this over with him, maybe with a bottle of wine between us.

What would be a bad enough idea in the first place is even worse now. We cannot. We should not.

A three-to-one win against the Rattlers makes things better. By the time the final horn sounds, I'm elated and my voice is hoarse from screaming my head off. "I'll tell you something." Corey winks at me as we make our way down the row once it's time to leave. "Whatever they're paying you isn't enough. You should ask for a raise."

She jerks her chin toward the ice, where Coach Kozak looks happy enough to burst. "I bet if you ask him right now, he'd give you part of his salary."

The funny part is, she's probably right. He's lucky I'm not a greedy woman.

At least, when it comes to money. When it comes to men… that's another story.

6

HARLOW

Ryder: I'm here. Where are you?

Me: I'm inside, at the bar. I ordered you a beer.

After sending the message, I set my phone down with a trembling hand. There's nothing to be worried about. We're far enough outside of town that the chances of anybody spotting us together are low, maybe nonexistent. He just finished an incredible game, and we're having dinner together to celebrate. Considering any and all fooling around is off the table with half of our group up in Seattle, it seems safe, going out together tonight. There's no risk of anybody catching us canoodling. And if anybody raises an eyebrow, we can fall back on the celebration angle. The team's season opener was a

huge success, in no small part thanks to the job
he did.

So what if my heart skips a beat when I catch sight
of him entering the restaurant? It's a cute place, the
kind with twinkling lights strung up in the trees and
bushes out front and soft, vaguely Italian music
piped in through discreetly placed speakers. In other
words, it would be a perfect date spot — and more
than a few couples have that idea, judging by the
looks of it. So the sight of him in a crisp button-
down shirt that matches his steely eyes has an almost
disappointing effect on me. I need to stay strong. We
made a promise that we wouldn't get physical.

Just like I made a promise to myself that nothing
would happen with him. Okay, so I haven't always
been true to my word, but I need to be now. Even if
he looks sinfully hot tonight.

"Hey." He runs a hand through his hair, still damp
after his post-game shower, then takes his pint glass
and gulps down maybe a third of the lager. "Oh, that
hits the spot."

"I thought for sure you would rather go out and
party tonight after that performance."

He almost looks insulted, his head snapping back so
he can give me a funny look. "Why would I do that?"

"I don't know. It sure seems like a lot of the team wanted to do that."

"Good for them. I'd rather be with you." There's a deeper meaning to his voice, and in the way he looks at me. Like he's hungry and I'm on the list of tonight's specials.

"As friends," I remind him.

"Sure, sure. You don't need to remind me." Right, but he doesn't need to be happy about it, I guess. He knows what's at stake just as well as I do. I don't want to hurt anybody, and neither does he.

It's not long before we are seated at a small two-top in the far corner of the dining room. I don't mind at all. The restaurant is awfully busy, but we're tucked away with a view of a beautifully landscaped back patio stretched out beyond the windows next to us. Those twinkling lights decorate potted plants and are strung along the railing overlooking a small pond. In other words, it's pretty romantic, but I have to keep a clear head. Maybe I should cool it on the wine, come to think of it. Nobody thinks clearly if they've had too much.

"I was so proud of you out there," I tell him once we place our orders. "You really stepped up. Everybody looked to you as a leader."

He gives me one of his patented smirks. "You're bullshitting me."

"I'm absolutely not. Maybe it's easier for me to see it, being an observer. But it's the truth. Everybody was looking to you tonight, and you rose to the occasion."

"Maybe I needed to step out of the shadows a little bit and prove what I'm capable of." He makes a big deal of staring down at his beer, his lips set in a thin line. It's so hard sometimes, separating my work from the private time I spend with him. I don't want to sit here and shrink him – and I doubt he would enjoy it if he knew I was. But it's like a reflex, taking what he says and analyzing it.

He feels overshadowed by Soren and Ash. Now that they're gone, he can shine. At least, that's how it sounds from where I'm sitting.

"What did the coach have to say?"

He chuckles. "He didn't say much of anything coherent. He was too busy slapping me on the back and laughing like he just won the lottery out of nowhere."

"He did look like he was ready to burst after the game was over."

"I think he finally sees things coming together."

"And he was awfully worried about how the lines would hold up without —" Dammit. I bite my tongue, but it's too late. He knows what I was thinking.

"Yeah, what a surprise the team didn't fall apart without them."

"I didn't mean it that way."

"Sure, you did. And I get it. You don't have to apologize or anything. They are the team stars, or else why would they have been called up?"

"Well, like you said, this is your chance to shine. Nobody can argue with stats. You've already got two assists on the record. There's nowhere to go from here but up."

"I wish I was as confident as you."

It's sort of annoying when our entrées arrive, since it means pausing the conversation until we're alone again. Once the server hurries off, I lean in a little. "What do you mean? You don't agree with me?"

He only grunts before waving a dismissive hand. "Don't listen to me. I don't know what the problem is tonight. You're right, I should be over the moon. You must think I sound like a little bitch."

"I don't think that at all. But I do want you to be happy."

Finally, his expression softens. "You know, I believe it. How do you do that?"

"Do what?"

"You're so sincere. Most people, they say something like that, but it's like, sure. Whatever you say." He rolls his eyes. "Not you. Something like that comes out of your mouth, and I believe you mean it."

"Maybe because I do. And I guess you must trust me. That's why you can believe me."

"Yeah, I guess so."

After we've tucked into our meals – linguine with Bolognese for me, steak for him – he gives me a little insight into what was going on with the team during the game. "Honestly, it was like playing with a different team from last year. There was so much more communication. Like, I could sense what Danny needed from me to score that goal. I knew where he'd be. I wish we could have played like that all along."

"You can thank your coach for that. He's the one who figured out the chemistry was off and put me in charge of mixing things up based on strengths and weaknesses, plus chemistry on the ice."

"Chemistry, huh?" The wicked gleam in his eyes both excites and disappoints me. He knows he shouldn't be talking like that right now.

And he must see the disappointment on my face, because he sits up a little straighter like he just got caught doing something naughty. "Sorry. Bad habit?"

"Yeah, but let's work on keeping that to a minimum, okay?"

"So how did it feel for you? Watching an actual game."

"Honestly, it was so exciting." I can't help but giggle when I remember the rush. "And it was so cool, seeing everything come together. I mean, Coach and I have worked for months to come up with, I don't know, the right recipe. I know that's not the right word, but that's sort of how it felt sometimes. Like we were two crazy cooks in the kitchen, throwing random things together to see if they work."

"I guess you make a good combination. No wonder he's so glad you started with the team." He winks before lifting his glass in my direction. "For the record, so am I."

"I sort of got the idea." I lift my glass to him. "Here's to you. Really, you killed it today."

"Let's just hope the rest of the season goes as well as this game." We toast to that, then spend the rest of dinner chatting about nothing in particular. But it's nice, just talking and getting to know each other better. There's no pressure, and since we both know there's a limit to how far we can go, it's sort of freeing. There's no expectations. No discomfort.

At least, there's no discomfort until it's time to go. I insist on paying, since this is supposed to be a celebration dinner in his honor, and he insists on walking me to my car. When we reach the driver's side door, I turn to him wearing a tight smile. "This is very nice. I'm really glad we got to spend some time together."

"Me, too." His eyes keep turning toward my mouth. Subconscious? I'm not sure. Either way, I can you tell exactly what he's thinking before he leans down.

And I pull back, shaking my head. "You know we can't do that right now."

His shoulders slump, and for one brief moment, so brief I might've imagined it, his eyes go narrow. It passes so quickly, it might not have happened at all. But I think it did. "I know. You're right."

"I better get going."

"Wait." It's a barely audible plea. He finds my hand with one of his and strokes my knuckles with his thumb. "That's it? The night's over?"

"You know it is."

"I'm not talking about anything physical. I was… Sort of hoping I could sleep over, anyway. As a friend."

7

RYDER

leaʒe ʒay yeʒ. Pleaʒe ʒay yeʒ. I'm holding my breath — it's pathetic, but I'm actually holding my breath waiting for her to answer. Hoping it will be the answer I want. I don't care what she makes me promise. I will promise anything right now, so long as I don't have to say goodbye to her. Not yet. Not when I've spent a week thinking about her, missing her, wanting her. I've earned this. I've been a good boy and kept my hands off her, and I deserve a little bit of a reward.

"Seriously?" She gives me one of her crooked smirks and looks me up and down. "Do you expect me to believe that?"

"I would even sleep on top of the covers if you want me to. I'll be a good boy. I promise."

"Sure. It's easy for you to say that now."

"What, you don't think I can control myself? You're so hot I won't be able to do anything but ravish you?"

Even in a dimly lit parking lot, I can see the flash of color that floods her cheeks. "Oh, God! I didn't mean it like that!"

"I know you didn't. I'm just busting your balls."

"Yeah, well, I don't have balls. Remember?"

"I remember." I bite my lip, staring at her.

"Ryder, please stop making this harder than it has to be."

Hearing her say that shouldn't make me as happy as it does. It's knowing she's fighting it, too. That I'm not the only one wishing we could go someplace and tear each other's clothes off. It doesn't make this sudden abstinence any easier to deal with, but it's not quite as miserable if I know she's still thinking about me that way. I'm not in this alone.

"Really. I won't push the envelope, I swear. I was sort of hoping we could spend some time together. That's all."

"And dinner wasn't enough?"

"You're like potato chips. I can't stop at just one."

"Oh, my God. Is that one of your best lines?"

"Depends. Did it work?"

That gets her. A giggle bubbles up out of her chest before she can stop it – even the hand she clamps over her mouth doesn't do any good. "Fine," she groans. "You can come and sleep over. But we both have to wear clothes."

"Boxer briefs are clothes, aren't they?"

She narrows her eyes – she wouldn't if she knew how hot she looks that way. "Sure, sure. You are trouble."

"I never pretended to be anything else, did I?" I'm not fooled. She likes that I'm trouble. There's a part of her that's turned on by how much trouble I am. "Meet you there?" I ask while backing away.

"Yeah. Meet you there."

"No more roommate?"

"Oh, no. Didn't I tell you? Corey moved out a couple of weeks ago. She has a place of her own now."

I can't say I'm sorry, even if Corey seems like a nice girl. It would be a little too awkward, trying to come up with a reason for me being there. "Cool. See you soon." As far as I'm concerned, the car can't move fast enough. I am hopelessly caught up in this woman. She'll never understand how just about everything I do is wrapped up in her.

Soren and Ash might be living it up in Seattle, hanging out with pros, doing what I want more than almost anything to do. But they're not sharing Harlow's bed tonight, are they? That's for me and me alone. If they find out, I won't pretend to be sorry, either. I'll be a good boy – there won't be anything to apologize for. And not because it would hurt their feelings or whatever. It would hurt her. And I can't stand it when she looks at me all disappointed and sad.

I guess that's the thing about finding somebody you really care about. Maybe I just never did before. I never knew a woman whose opinion matters as much as hers. I've never known one I wanted to share so much with, either. Something about her makes me open up. I want to be honest. I want her to know me.

It's kind of scary, but in a good way. Like in those final moments before the puck drops. There's nothing but adrenaline and excitement and sure, everything could go completely to hell for so many reasons — but it could also be incredible, like it was today. When everything clicked and we were all in the zone together, putting to use what we learned in the off-season.

And we did it without the so-called stars. That feels pretty good, too.

I make it to the house before she does. I guess I'm even more eager than I thought, because I sit with my fingers tapping the wheel, wishing she would hurry up and get here. I let out a sigh of relief when her headlights appear down the street.

I promise to be good. I promise to be good. I have to remember that as we meet by her front door, or otherwise I might do something hopelessly stupid like grab a hold of her, throw her over my shoulder, and march up to the bedroom.

Instead of doing that, she cracks open a bottle of wine pulled from the fridge. "Sorry, I don't have any beer."

"Wine is fine."

"Why don't you sit on the couch? Maybe find some music to put on." If I didn't know better, I would think she's trying to set the mood. I'm going to give her more credit than that. She is a hostess trying to make her guest comfortable. I keep that in mind as I pull up her Spotify account through her Smart TV.

"Your taste in music is… eclectic."

"What does that mean?"

"It means you've got showtunes, hip-hop, and classic rock all on the same playlist."

"I have wide and varied tastes. Is that a crime?"

"No. Last time I checked, it's not a crime." It is, however, adorable. Maybe that's just because I like her so much.

When she sits on the other end of the sofa, silence falls between us. It's a little awkward, to put it mildly. Wanting to touch her. Knowing I shouldn't. Feeling like she wants me to, but knows it would be a mistake. Still, I can't ignore the electricity in the air, and I doubt she can, either. It's so thick, I can hardly breathe.

"I wonder if I'll get any trick-or-treaters this year."

An interesting lead off, but it's probably the safest topic, all things considered. "First year in the new house and all that."

"Yeah. I know there are kids around— I saw them during summer break but of course, now they're back in school. I guess I'll have to get some candy just in case. It might actually be fun. I didn't have a chance to do much of that when I was in the apartment."

"You should dress up, too."

"That's a good idea, actually." She frowns, pursing her lips. "I haven't dressed up for Halloween in as long as I can remember. What could I dress up as?"

"A sexy doctor?" She rolls her eyes. "I mean, you already have the costume, right?"

"You are absolutely incorrigible."

"Hey. No physical stuff, but that doesn't mean I can't flirt a little. What can I say? You bring it out in me." Let her pretend to disapprove all she wants. I see the smile she can't hide.

I want her to do more than smile. I want her to scream my name. I want her nails scraping against my scalp and down my back. I want to drive home tomorrow morning with her scent on my skin.

But when she yawns and stretches, I know it's time for bed. I see the questions in her eyes. I sense her hesitation. "I'll be a good boy, I promise. Besides, the game kicked my ass today." That's not totally true, but it seems to give her a little comfort, so I'll let her believe it. Some things, a man fights through. I could have both legs in a cast and I would still want her riding on top of me.

I have to settle for getting undressed and crawling into bed, hoping this isn't as impossible as it seems like it will be. Especially once she's down to a tank top and yoga pants. Not the sexiest outfit in the world, but on her, it's a bigger turn-on than any lingerie I can imagine.

"Goodnight," she murmurs, giving me a peck on the cheek before rolling onto her side with her back to me. It's a matter of reflex, the way my arm snakes around her. How am I going to lie here all night and not at least hold her?

She stiffens for a second and I hold my breath until she relaxes and settles against me.

And right away, the second her ass touches my crotch, I know this was a big mistake. She's counting on me – I have to do right by her. But dammit, I'm only human. And usually, when a woman's ass presses against my dick, it means we're about to have fun.

She goes as stiff as I'm now becoming. "Is that what I think it is?" she whispers in the darkness.

What does she expect? All I can do is remember being with her in this bed and how incredible it was. "No. I brought the broom up from the kitchen."

"Okay, you're big, but not quite that big."

"Is it a problem?" I pull my hips back, even though I don't want to.

"No. I mean, it's not like I'm not… excited."

Fuck me. How can this possibly end in anything other than disaster? I mean, I'm sure it wouldn't feel like a disaster at the time, but it would end up being one. "We should just go to sleep, I guess." She shivers when my breath hits the back of her neck and dammit, I have never had to wrestle with self-control like I do now. Knowing she wants me the way I want her. It's better if we both go to sleep, and quick.

Somehow, I manage it, since the next thing I know there's a gasp that breaks me out of a deep sleep.

It wasn't Harlow's gasp, either. She's just waking up, too, propping herself up on her elbow and looking toward the door.

Where Corey stands with a box of donuts balanced on one hand and her jaw hanging halfway to the floor.

8

HARLOW

Crap. Crap, crap, crap.

I'm dreaming, right? This is my guilty conscience manifesting my fears in the form of a stomach dropping, nausea inducing nightmare. In real life, this wouldn't happen, would it? I wouldn't wake up to find Corey standing in my room, holding a box of donuts. Of all things. It's too surreal.

But I feel Ryder behind me. I even feel his morning wood pressing into my lower back until he sort of scoots away like he wants to prove to Corey there's nothing going on. Like she didn't walk in on anything.

Something tells me it doesn't matter.

Her mouth is hanging open and her body is frozen like she's in shock. "Corey," I whisper, trembling.

That seems to snap her out of it. She stands up straighter, blinking rapidly. "I'm sorry. I'll, uh, get out of here." She's already down the hall before I can take a breath, and soon her footsteps patter down the stairs. I half expect her to bolt out the front door, but she doesn't — at least, I don't hear anything that sounds like it.

"Oh, my God." I drop back onto my pillow and bunch it up around my face. Maybe if I close my eyes tight enough and wish this away, everything will be alright. I can go back to the point in my life where my friend didn't walk in on me and a man I should not be sleeping with.

"I'm sorry." Ryder gives my shoulder an awkward pat. "I must've been out cold. I didn't hear her come in."

"Neither did I." The memory flashes across my mind's eye, and I remember giving her a key when she was staying here. Silly me, not imagining that backfiring at any point.

"What do you want me to do?" All of the usual brashness is gone, replaced by concern. At least he sees how monumental this is. At least he's not making a joke out of it.

"Can you turn back time and get out of here before she shows up?" I haven't heard the front door open and close, so I'm assuming she's still around. "I can't believe this. Of all the stupid ways for somebody to find out…"

The ironic part is, nothing actually happened. All we did was sleep. But considering Ryder's in nothing but his underwear, it can't look good from Corey's perspective.

"You know, the longer we hang out in here, the worse this looks."

He's absolutely right. "I guess we need to face the music." No idea has ever appealed to me less, but I can't run and hide. Ryder pulls his clothes on while I grab my bathrobe and slide into it. A quick glimpse of my reflection in the mirror confirms I don't have sex hair or anything like that— nothing about my appearance could give her the impression I'm trying to hide something.

Maybe I should try to stop trembling.

She's in the kitchen fixing coffee when I reach the bottom of the stairs. Right away, she blurts out, "I'm so sorry. I only brought the donuts over as a thank you for helping me. I didn't notice the other car sitting out front. I'm such an idiot."

"You're not an idiot. You couldn't have known."

She's about to say something else, but Ryder's entrance cuts her off. "Hi," she murmurs, and the way she blushes only makes things worse. I want to crawl into a hole, I swear.

"Hey." He shoots me a questioning look — as if I have the first clue how to navigate this situation. She hasn't screamed or pointed fingers or called anybody names, so I'm guessing that means she's okay with what she found upstairs. *Please, let her be okay with it.* Otherwise, this could get ugly.

"Are you hungry?" She nudges the donuts his way. "Please, help yourself."

Could this be more awkward? "Thanks."

"I hope you don't mind me coming in unannounced." She fishes the key out of her pocket and plops it on the counter. "I guess I should give this back to you while I'm thinking about it."

"I honestly don't mind you having it — it's kind of nice knowing somebody could come over here if I needed them to."

"Okay, cool."

Yet another awkward silence falls over us. I want to scream, I really do. This is so painfully awkward.

"I better go." Ryder lifts his donut on his way toward the door. "See you later." I sort of wish he wouldn't leave me alone, but I understand why he wants to go. I almost wish I could go with him.

He's barely out the door before Corey practically jumps on me. "Oh, my God!" she gasps. "Since when? No, let me guess. It happened in Seattle. I knew it!"

"Calm down." I'm starting to get a headache. I rub my temples, but it's no use. "Nothing happened. He just slept here."

"Sure, sure."

"I'm serious. He slept over. That's it. We went out to get something to eat after the game and came back here, but all we did was sleep."

"Hey, no judgment here, either way. You don't have to explain yourself to me."

"I still feel like I should." I also feel like I should shove a donut into my mouth. Stress eating has always been a problem for me. The fact that I chose a Boston cream almost makes me cringe after I've taken a bite. I only know one person from Boston, and he just walked out of here.

"Listen, don't feel like you have to explain yourself or apologize to me. I don't see anything wrong with you having a relationship with whoever you want to have a relationship with."

"You would probably be the only person who feels that way. That's the problem."

"So, I won't tell anybody. It's pretty simple, right?"

"I wish it were that simple. I feel... less-than-ethical."

"Ethics, shmethics."

"That's easy for you to say."

Her face falls a little before she nods. "Yeah, you're right. I have no business being so blasé. I'm sorry."

"You're just trying to be supportive. You don't have to apologize." Strange how finishing the donut did nothing to calm my nerves. Maybe a second one will help.

"For what it's worth, I did knock on the front door before I came in. I guess you were... worn out?" She bites her lip to hide a smile and fails horribly.

"Knock it off."

"Sorry, sorry. I really think it's cool. I guess I'm just excited for you."

"That's really sweet of you. And I don't mean to sound so negative or angry or whatever. I'm just worried. And I don't feel great about myself."

"I'm telling you, you have nothing to worry about from me. You deserve to have somebody in your life. And if you're going to take a chance and have him sleep over, that must mean you really care about him. Otherwise, it wouldn't be worth it."

She's right about that, for sure. "I just wish everybody felt about it the way you do."

9

ASH

"You gave it your all out there today."

Oh, God. Not that. That might be the one thing I want less than anything else to hear. It's not so much the words my mother says, but how she says them. She's obviously trying to comfort me in any way she can, and it makes me feel like a complete loser.

"Of course, he did." Dad pats my shoulder while we wait for a table to open up at the bistro where I was thinking I'd take my family out to dinner after the game, sort of a celebration. Maybe I was feeling a little full of myself when we made these arrangements. I mean, who wouldn't look forward to their family watching them play for a major league hockey team? When I look back on how much I anticipated this, I feel like the world's biggest tool.

Then again, who imagines themselves screwing up like I did? If I had played blindfolded, I couldn't have done much worse. My big shot, and I'm blowing it.

I'm surprised they want to be seen in public with me.

My parents turn toward each other and talk over something or other, which is when my sister elbows me in the ribs. "You could try not looking like you swallowed glass."

I can be honest with her. There's not much need to put on a happy face. "I didn't invite you guys up from Newport Beach to watch me play like a rookie."

"You sort of are, though. Aren't you? You've never played in the NHL before."

"You know what I mean. I might as well have been handling a stick for the first time ever."

She rolls eyes that look a lot like mine. "It wasn't that bad. You're being too hard on yourself."

But that's the thing. I'm not. I am downright disturbed at how off I was today. My reflexes were shit, I was a step behind everybody else on the team.

Amy has always been a reasonable person, so it shouldn't surprise me when her head tips to the side and she furrows her brow like she's thinking. "Maybe it was nerves? Knowing we were there?"

"Yeah, you're probably right. I got all up in my head."

"You wouldn't be the first athlete to get up in their head, you know. Don't be so hard on yourself."

That's easy for her to say. As far as she knows, I only screwed up today. She doesn't know that this is the third game in a row that I've botched. Sure, we won them – I have that going for me. This would all be so much worse if the team had lost. But I wasn't the one that led them to victory, that's for sure. All I did was hold them back.

I'm going to be sent back down. I know it. It's like there's an ax poised over my head, held up by the thinnest thread. It won't take much for that thread to snap. All I can do until that happens is live in dread.

At dinner, it's better that I ask for all the details on Amy's life. She just started her freshman year at UCLA, so she's got plenty of stories to tell. I can sense my parents' concern, though. They keep exchanging the sort of knowing glances parents do when they suspect something is up, but I do my best to cheerfully ignore them. I don't want to talk about me. I don't want them to know how full of doubt I've become.

Finally, while we're waiting for dessert, Mom blurts out what she's clearly been dying to ask all night. "Are you unhappy? Are you having trouble adjusting?"

"I had a bad game. That's all."

"It didn't look that way from where we sat." Dad lifts a shoulder when I shoot him a sharp look. "It's true. You're being too hard on yourself, son."

"Exactly what I said," Amy agrees. "Okay, so you didn't live up to your standards. But your standards are, like, ridiculously high as it is."

"They sort of have to be. This is the real deal. This isn't practice. I'm playing in the NHL."

"Which must mean you're doing something right." Mom gives me a pat on my arm that I guess is supposed to make me feel better. Right now, I only feel patronized. They don't know what they're talking about, anyway. I know they're trying to make me feel better, and when you're trying to make somebody feel better, you say all kinds of random things that might not even be true. At the end of the day, none of them understands. They've watched countless games over the years – they're supportive, and always have been. But they still don't know what it's like to be out there chasing a puck and feeling like everything's slipping away no matter how hard they try to hold onto their dream.

Once I'm alone in my hotel room and the family has gone to their own suite, I can relax a little. I don't have the feeling that I need to put on a happy face for anybody. It's a relief, since pretending can be exhausting. I'm more worn out from that than from the game when I flop back on the bed and pull out my phone. There's only one person I want to talk to right now, maybe the only person who can understand what I'm going through and even give me a few tips on how to get through it. That's her job, right?

Besides, I miss the hell out of her and it's been a few days since we last talked. The sense of loneliness that's haunted me ever since arriving here is stronger than ever as I pull her up and place a FaceTime call.

Any momentary dread that she's not available fades away when she answers wearing a huge smile. "Hey, stranger! How's it going up there? You had a game today, right? Congrats on the win!"

It shouldn't be a surprise, hearing that she keeps up with the team. "Thanks. But between you and me, I had nothing to do with it."

"What do you mean?" She's at her place, I see, in her home office.

"You know what, it looks like you're in the middle of something. We don't have to talk about this —"

"Like hell, we don't. Tell me what's going on. You seem upset."

"Not upset. Not exactly." If I can't open up to her, who can I open up to? It would be stupid to push her away right now, when it's clear she wants to help. I need to get over the sense of embarrassment.

"They have me on left wing."

"I know. How's it going, transitioning to defense?"

"That's just it. I fucking suck at it."

She tips her head to the side like she always does when she's thinking. "I've seen you play. You are a naturally gifted player."

"I'll try to keep that in mind when I'm busy losing pucks to forechecking in the neutral zone."

"Why do you think that's happening? And don't tell me it's because you suck – we both know you do not suck. So why are you getting in your own way?"

"Is that what I'm doing?"

"You tell me." She chews her lip and God, I wish I were the one chewing that lip right now. I wish we were together, without all this bullshit. Did I think I wanted this? Why? So I can doubt every aspect of my game? So I can wonder what the hell I'm doing here in the first place? Was I fooling myself all along? Kidding myself into believing I had something I don't? It's very easy to feel like you're hot shit when you're a big fish in a small pond. And that's what I've been since I signed with the team. A big fish, thinking he would be better off in a larger body of water. How wrong could I have been?

"Well?" she prods gently. "Why are you doing this? Why is everything falling apart?"

"Maybe I'm not as ready as I thought I was."

"Or…" She gives me a gentle smile. "You're coming up with reasons why this won't work. Maybe you feel uncomfortable playing at this level. There's nothing wrong with that. You would not be the first person to get what they wanted and find out it's a much bigger undertaking than they could've imagined."

"I don't have time for that. Getting cold feet or whatever. I can't let that happen."

"You're a human being, not a machine. Everybody goes through growing pains. Everybody deals with self-doubt."

"Not me."

"Then congratulations, because you would be the first person living to never experience self-doubt." She leans a little closer to her screen, but of course, that's not close enough. Until she's by my side, it'll never be close enough. "Do yourself a favor and get out of your own way. That's the only way you can get through this, and I know you can do it. I've seen what you're capable of – whether you want to admit that right now or not. I understand why you don't. You're feeling down on yourself. Remember why you play the game in the first place. You're good at it, and it's fun. It can still be fun. Maybe you have to allow it to be, you know? You don't have to take this so deadly serious. If you're up in your head all the time, you'll never be able to get into your flow – and that's where you thrive."

The more she talks, the more sure I am that being up in my head isn't my only problem. No doubt it's one problem, sure. I wouldn't be the first athlete to fuck up because they can't stop overthinking their game.

There's another, much bigger issue that I'm only now starting to wake up to.

I just want to be with her.

And I'm starting to wonder if I might be sabotaging myself so I can get back home.

10

ASH

"Hey."

It's not what the girl says, but the way she says it that tells me this isn't the first time she's tried to get my attention. It's not easy getting somebody's attention in a loud club like this, with so much noise and loud music and overlapping voices.

But that's not the problem, and I know it. I know it even as I stare down at her and wonder why I ever used to like coming out to places like this. It's like I was a different person, and not very long ago, either.

She offers a cute smile. "Why are you standing here all alone?" She nods toward the dance floor, where a certain hockey player I'm best friends with is dancing with a redhead who keeps grinding her ass against him. "I thought you came in with him."

"I did."

"And I thought her friend tried to get you to dance."

I tip my head to the side, studying the petite blonde. "Are you stalking me?"

Her cheeks flush before she laughs. "No, just curious. You sort of caught my attention. But you're not like all the other guys in here, that's why I couldn't stop watching you."

Not like the other guys. I don't think I've ever heard that one before. "How do you mean?"

Something tells me she's not in this for a deep conversation, but she answers easily enough. "You're not prowling around the room, seeing if you can score with any of the girls. You're not hitting on anything with two legs and boobs."

I like her. She's smart, and she's honest. That's kind of refreshing after having women practically crawling on me every time we go out after a game.

Jesus. Since when is that a problem? I'm turning into a bitter old man way before my time.

"I guess I'm just not into it," I tell her with a shrug. I mean, what's the alternative? Pouring my heart out?

I doubt she's in the mood to hear my petty problems. Like how much I miss Harlow, the woman who's not my girlfriend, but is much more than an acquaintance or even a casual hook up. We never did decide what to call ourselves, did we? If she's our girlfriend, are we her boyfriends? No, if anything, our relationship feels too special to use some random, safe words to describe it.

"That's a shame. I was going to ask you if you want to dance." She looks down at my feet, then back up at me. "You haven't stopped tapping your foot."

"Okay, now you're starting to freak me out a little." But I'm laughing for the first time all night, which has to be a good thing. I have been wanting to dance — not like it's one of my favorite pastimes or anything, but the music is good. It's only that I wish Harlow were here to dance with. I doubt you could pull me off the floor if she were here and wanted to get out there and shake her ass.

"Okay, let's go." I follow her onto the floor and make it a point to catch Soren's eye. The wry smirk he wears leaves a bad taste in my mouth, but I brush it off. He doesn't mean anything by it, no matter how much it looks like he's sort of gloating. I can almost read his mind. I thought you weren't into it.

I'm not, that's the thing. Being here makes me feel like I'm cheating. Harlow is home, waiting for us.

What does it make us if we're out flirting with other women, buying them drinks, dancing with them? He can say it's innocent all he wants – and it could be, it really could. But intent matters, too. The feeling like we're bending the rules by doing this. I shouldn't have let him talk me into coming to the club, but then I didn't like the idea of him going out alone, either. I hate feeling like I have to keep an eye on him, but that's exactly what went through my head when he said I didn't have to come with him.

The blonde is cute, and she's a good dancer. It's a shame she's not dancing with a man who wants to be with her. I try to put on a good show though, but it's awkward, trying to keep space between our bodies. I made a promise. I haven't always kept my promises in the past, but this time I want to. It's important.

That's what's going through my head as I glance across the floor, finding Soren and his redhead in the crowd. She's turned around to face him now, and if she were any closer, she'd be wearing his clothes. She has one hand on his chest and the other around the back of his neck while his hand wanders dangerously close to her ass. She pulls down and he goes along with her, until their noses touch.

It doesn't take a genius to know what's going to happen next.

"Excuse me. Sorry." I don't wait to see the blonde's reaction before breaking away from her and making my way across the floor. "Hey. I need to talk to you."

The way his face falls and his eyes roll, it's pretty obvious he's not happy about being interrupted. "Sorry," he tells the girl before sighing and following me off the dance floor. As soon as we are closer to the bar, I turn on him, even shoving him a little when I see his smirk.

"What the hell is wrong with you? What do you think you're doing?"

"Last I checked, I was dancing. So were you, remember?"

"No. Don't do that. I wasn't dancing the way you were."

"Oh, so there's a difference now?"

"You know damn well there is. Don't be cute. Don't act like you don't know exactly what I'm saying. We made a promise, remember?"

"I remember." He couldn't sound less impressed. "And last I checked, I'm honoring that promise."

"Technically. But not really."

"You're not my mother, Ash. Stop acting like it."

"Then stop pretending you have any interest in being true to Harlow."

His head snaps back before he folds his arms. I've seen that hard look in his eyes, but usually he's looking at an opponent. Not at me, his best friend. I'm usually an observer, not the subject.

"You're serious. aren't you?" He laughs, and the sound is like nails on a chalkboard. "Get real. What, you think she's not screwing around with Ryder? Do you think they didn't sleep together the second we were gone? Give me a break."

"Don't even say that."

"Too late. I did. And you're fooling yourself if you think they're not —"

I'm not going to wait for him to say it again. Once was bad enough.

"Fuck off!" And then, because I've completely lost my mind, I do something I never imagined doing. To anybody else, but not to him. And not in a club full of people.

My right fist pulls back, then pistons forward before I know what I'm doing. The satisfying contact it makes with Soren's jaw almost makes it worthwhile, and a rush of satisfaction races through me when his head snaps to the side and he stumbles backward.

He recovers quickly, touching a hand to the spot where I made contact, and at first he smiles.

Then, he hits me back. Pain explodes across the side of my face when he strikes my cheekbone – not hard enough to break it, but enough that I'll feel it in the morning. "The fuck is your problem?" he bellows, while everybody around us backs away.

"Your fucking attitude is my problem!" I shove him with both hands, and he glances off a high-top table before throwing himself at me, driving me back against the bar. I barely register the shouts of surprise and fear around us. All I know is, he's going to pay for this. I'm going to make him pay.

At least, that's what my stupid, alcohol-soaked brain thinks until a pair of very large hands take me by the shoulders and pry me away from Soren, who is also being handled by a bouncer. "Out, both of you!" the bartender shouts, and I barely have time to react before the two of us are being hauled out of the club by our necks.

No way this doesn't get back to the team, to both teams.

No way it doesn't get back to Harlow.

Even more than that. No way are we ever going to be the same after this.

ASH

What am I doing? Standing here, nervous as hell, pressing my finger to the doorbell and listening as it chimes inside the house. It's barely seven in the morning and probably way too early for a visitor, but I didn't exactly think this through. This entire trip was planned at the spur of the moment.

The first of my worries was cleared when I pulled up in my Uber and found no other cars besides Harlow's parked in the driveway. I see now how worried I was. My eyes were peeled for Ryder's car – it's not exactly the kind of thing you could overlook or mistake for someone else's. It's not here. He's not with her.

Maybe she's not here. Ever consider that? She could've gotten a ride somewhere and not come home yet, which would explain her car's presence. Maybe she spent the night at his place.

Then I hear her and see her shadow moving behind the curtain in front of the door's glass cut-out. When she pulls the curtain inside, her eyes go wide the way I knew they would. She flings the door open fast enough that she's still in the middle of gasping by the time we're face-to-face. "What are you doing here?" she squeals before jumping into my outstretched arms.

And all at once, everything's alright. Everything slides into place. She's where she belongs, in my arms, and I can hold her close to me and inhale her light, floral shampoo, and the unique scent of her skin, still warm from bed.

"I had to see you. It's been torture."

"I didn't think you were allowed to leave!" She pulls back, her eyes darting over my face. Eyes that go narrow right away. "What happened to your face?"

She raises her fingers to the fresh bruise on my cheekbone but doesn't make contact. "Oh, you know," I joke. "Got a little too feisty during practice. It's no big deal."

Does she buy the excuse? I'm not sure. I don't think so. "Are you okay?"

"Fine. Just fine."

"But what about —"

"I had the day off, and I've already booked my flight back tonight. No, I'm technically not supposed to leave town, but what my coach doesn't know won't hurt him." I realize I'm practically holding my breath while I wait for her to absorb this. "You won't tell on me, will you?"

"What do you think, dork?" Her brilliant smile eases the tightness in my chest before she hugs me again. "Only one day, huh?"

"Less than that. Maybe twelve hours."

"Then I guess we'd better make the most of the time we have together."

Because I'm only human, my dick twitches at the suggestion. But no, we're not supposed to do that. That's not what she meant.

Unfortunately.

Instead of taking her to bed, I wait for her to get dressed so we can go for breakfast at a café in town. It's early enough that the odds of anyone seeing us together are low — something she still worries about, her gaze sweeping the room before we take our seats. She even wears a ball cap pulled low over her eyes like she's trying to go incognito.

"So? How's it been, really? Since the last time we talked. Have you been feeling any better?"

There is so much open, honest concern radiating from her. It shines from her eyes as they sparkle my way. Would it be too much to ask for us to sit and stare at each other for a while? I don't need to talk. I just need to be in her presence.

It's not going to be that easy. "I'm trying to get over the stuff we talked about."

"Have you been able to identify any areas where you might be sabotaging yourself?"

Something about the question stirs a flash of anger deep inside. I see Soren's face in front of me. That knowing smirk. "You know what? I don't want to talk about that. Tell me about you. How have you been? I understand you're kicking ass down here."

"The way you make it sound, you'd think I was playing in the games."

"You might not be on skates, but you're there on the ice."

"You give me too much credit."

"The team's done nothing but win so far this season. When do you think was the last time that happened? Last season, it took eight games for us to get our first win, and even that one was by the skin of our teeth."

She only waves a hand and starts building her lox and cream cheese bagel using some of the extras the server brought over to make a decent looking sandwich. "Well, it's been good, like you said. Things have been going smoothly."

"And what about you, personally?" It's not easy to be playful when what I want is to know whether she's been spending time with Ryder. I can't come out and blurt the question. I'd only end up coming off childish and suspicious. She doesn't deserve that.

"Personally?" She takes a bite and chews slowly. "I've been missing you. Is that what you want to know?"

"Maybe." I nudge her foot under the table and she nudges back. It is impossible not to flirt with this woman.

"Congratulations. I missed you, like you knew I would. Both of you."

Both of us. Me, and the best friend who gave me this bruise on my face last night. Maybe that's why I was in such a hurry to get down here, too. I needed to see her before she found out about it. Obviously, she hasn't yet — it's barely been eight hours since the fight.

"What were your plans for today?" I ask after paying the check. "I'm not trying to get in the way of your day off."

"I was going to head over to the farmer's market, grab some fruits and veggies."

"Can I come with you?"

"Of course." Still, she gives me a funny look as we're leaving the restaurant. "Are you sure that's what you want to be doing with your day off?"

That doesn't matter. She doesn't get it. I could be anywhere, doing anything, and I'd be perfectly satisfied so long as we were together.

She grabs a couple of canvas totes from the trunk of her car once we've parked across from the park, where farmers and vendors have set up their tables. I've never really been the type of guy to spend his Saturday morning wandering around like this, but now that we're strolling up and down the rows, I can appreciate the change of pace. It's a beautiful day, brilliantly sunny, and the October air is a nice change from the summer's oppressive heat. It's still not anything like Seattle is right now, where it's been cloudy, cool and drizzling for days. "Do you think weather plays a part in how we handle things?"

She looks up from the jar of preserves she was studying. "You mean, like, can bad weather bring us down? Sure. Lots of people go through seasonal depression, for instance. When the nights get longer and there's less sunshine, or when there's a string of storms. It can definitely have an impact."

"I feel a lot better when the sun is on my skin."

"That's good." She screws up her mouth up like she's thinking something over. "I bet there's a way to get even more sun."

"What did you have in mind?"

Once we're finished shopping and back at her house, she shows me. "It almost feels weird, getting into the pool on my own instead of getting pushed in." I don't have a pair of trunks with me, so I settle for swimming in my shorts just in case any of her neighbors feel like taking a peek out their windows. I'm treading water by the time she joins me and lets her robe drop so I can get an eye full of her in a white bikini I would love to pull off with my teeth. *Down, boy.* I really want to do this right. I want a clear conscience.

It's enough to splash around for a while, to float on our backs and talk about everything and nothing at the same time. I can breathe here, with her. I see things for what they are — like Soren's attitude. He is all wrapped up in how new everything is now. How he's finally getting a taste of everything he wanted — and I guess he wasn't counting on it. He's still the same guy I've always known. A decent guy at heart, no doubt. I know he still cares for Harlow. That sort of thing doesn't go away overnight.

And I'm sure we'll be friends again. It will take time, but we'll be alright. It's easy to believe that when I'm here, and I'm happy, and there's nothing I have to do but enjoy myself. Even if the clock's ticking the entire time.

12

HARLOW

"I really would like you to meet them sometime. My family."

"Sure. I would love to." Because right now, floating in the water, nothing seems impossible. Not even the idea of us being able to easily explain our relationship to Ash's family. Like it would all be so normal, having dinner with his parents and his younger sister the way people do when they're in a relationship. Like there wouldn't be anything to hide.

"That wouldn't work, would it?" There's a touch of sadness in his voice, but he seems pretty good-natured about it, anyway. "Sometimes I get ahead of myself."

"I wouldn't want to lie about who I am to you."

"I know." Because, of course, even with Ryder and Soren not in the picture, it's still not a good idea for us to be together at all.

At least he sounds like he understands and isn't too bummed. I don't think I've ever seen him this relaxed and serious, but somehow lighthearted at the same time.

"I've missed this," he announces with a soft sigh.

"Hanging out at the pool?"

"Home. I missed home." He swims to the side of the pool and folds his arms on the edge, resting his chin on them.

"So you've been homesick."

"Like a kid at summer camp. That's pretty lame, isn't it?"

"I was thinking sweet." I approach slowly, cautiously. I don't want him to feel like I'm making a big deal about sharing his emotions. He might end up shutting down, and I don't want that.

He makes a pained face once I've reached his side. "Sweet? Why don't you just cut my balls off while you're at it?"

"I didn't know being sweet was such a crime." I fold my arms on the edge the way he has, kicking my feet up behind me and stirring up the water. He is an enigma, that much is for sure. Underneath the cool, smart-ass attitude is a tender heart. He only wants to protect it, and I understand why. The tender hearted are the easiest to hurt. And the last thing I want to do is hurt him, or anybody. I have to be careful.

"Anyway, I think that's part of what I've been dealing with. But only kids get homesick."

"That's not true. Don't be unfair to yourself. You have a beautiful home here, and friends, and people who care about you. Myself included, obviously."

"I definitely missed you."

"I've missed you, too. But think of it this way, if you weren't doing a great job up there, they would've sent you back by now." I tap him with my foot underwater. "So you can't be doing as bad as you think you are."

I am not imagining the shadow that passes over his face like a cloud passing in front of the sun. Not just any cloud. A storm cloud – his brows draw together, and his mouth purses until his lips are practically lost. What is he not telling me? I know if I call him out, this will end in disaster. We only have a few more hours together, and I don't want to ruin it by pushing too hard.

"I definitely miss this weather." He offers an empty little laugh as he changes the subject. "I already said that, didn't I?"

"It bears repeating." Then, I tap his shoulder before pushing away from the wall. "You're it."

"Oh, so that's the game we're playing?" Any hint of worry is lost when he lunges for me, and for a little while it's enough to play. To let go of everything and everyone else and focus on having fun. He's a lot quicker than I am in the water – his body is just more powerful – but I'm slippery, so it's not easy for him to catch me.

Though when he does, when he draws me close with his hands on my waist and his body pressed against mine, my willpower threatens to break. "You know we shouldn't," I murmur, pressing my hands against his shoulders.

"Yeah, yeah." He's still staring at my mouth, and I still like the way he stares. Every nerve in my body is tuned to him, to his slightest movement. I forget to breathe as he leans closer, his breath heating my face. One kiss won't hurt anything, right? Just one kiss to get rid of this ungodly tension.

All at once, Ryder's sweet, trusting face flashes across my mind's eye, and it's enough to harden my resolve. I'm not kidding around this time when I firmly push away from Ash, whose face falls a little when I do. "Come on. All this swimming made me hungry." It's a lot safer if we're out of the water and both fully clothed.

Once he's dried off and dressed, he joins me in the kitchen and puts together a salad using some of the produce we picked up earlier today while I grill chicken breasts to go along with it. While we cook, he asks questions about the team and how everybody's doing. I'm happy to be able to give him good news about everybody's progress. "Don't get me wrong. You're missed, and so is Soren. But they're doing their best to cover the loss."

"So I'm not exactly replaceable, but maybe a little?" He brings the chef's knife down on a head of romaine much harder than he needed to.

"You know that's not what I'm getting at. Here I am, trying to reassure you…"

He laughs it off, easing my concern. "I'm busting your balls. Of course, I'm glad everybody's doing well, and I know we have you to thank for that."

It's funny how my immediate knee-jerk reaction is to brush off the compliment. Why do I do that? Maybe I need to start treating myself the way I would a patient. Maybe it's time to delve into my brain a little and figure out why I do what I do. Maybe it's years of feeling like my accomplishments weren't quite as worthwhile compared to my brother. Maybe years of feeling overshadowed made me create this defense mechanism where I try not to take myself too seriously.

instead of brushing him off, I grit my teeth and smile. "I hope so. I really hope everybody's learning skills they can take with them over the season."

"I'll give you one thing." He drags a cucumber slice through a blob of ranch dressing before popping it into his mouth. "You're diplomatic when you're trying to figure out how to take a compliment for once."

"It's not easy for me! Don't forget, this is my first job out of school. I never want to sound too sure of myself. Like I'm bragging or anything."

"When you're around me, you can brag." I narrow my eyes at him and he only laughs. "What? I'm trying to be supportive. Give me a break."

I wish we could stay like this all night, joking, talking about nothing in particular. There's no pressure, there's no awkwardness. I hate the idea of him leaving already, especially when it seems like he needed this. A short break, time spent with somebody who cares about him. Once again, I want to ask about Soren and how they're handling this new situation together... but something stops me. I don't know what it is. A sixth sense, I guess. I've spent enough time with him to know when he has something on his mind he's not ready to discuss.

So, even though I want to point out that he has his best friend in Seattle with him, I don't bother. Whatever is dragging him down isn't the sort of thing a best friend can help with, I guess. It's not like I can't understand or relate. There's only so much Ruby was able to do for my morale when I first found out about Kyle, for instance. Sure, it was great to have a cheering section at my back, but she couldn't deal with the feelings for me. I had to go through that myself. And I came out stronger on the other side – at least, I like to think I did. I guess it's kind of like when a baby bird hatches – they have to break out of the shell themselves. As much as a bystander might want to help, it wouldn't really be helpful in the long run.

That's what is still on my mind as I take Ash to the airport. "You sure you're not going to get in trouble for this?" I ask once we're out of the car near the gate.

"Positive, or else I wouldn't have risked it. Don't worry so much."

"How can I help it?" Now that it's time to say goodbye, I can't find the words. I don't want him to go, not when today was so bright and fun.

More than that, it gave my soul something I didn't realize I was missing until now. Like part of me went away, but I had it back for a little while. Now I'm going to have to adjust all over again.

I already suspected I was in too deep with him, but now I'm sure. I have fallen too hard.

So hard, in fact, that I can't bring myself to pull away when he takes my face in his hands. I need his touch too much.

"There's something I have to tell you. I've been debating all day on whether I should admit this."

"What's wrong?" I search his face for any clue, but his expression is unreadable. He looks worried, that's all I know, so of course I worry, too.

"I…" his voice falters for a second, but he clears his throat and lowers his brow like he's determined to push through whatever wants to hold him back. "I love you."

Well, damn. Not what I was expecting, not by a long shot.

"You don't have to say it back," he's quick to add, shaking his head. "I don't expect it. But that's what brought me down here today. Being without you — it's so obvious to me now. When I'm not with you, it's like all the color has been drained out of the world. Even getting something I thought I wanted... Somehow, it doesn't feel as good, because it means being away from you."

"I hope I haven't ruined anything for you."

"Not even close. Knowing you're here, waiting... it'll make the inevitable a little easier to deal with." We both know Seattle isn't permanent. Eventually he'll come home, and so will Soren, and we can all be together again.

"But I couldn't get on that plane without telling you. I would kick myself to death by the time we landed. I hope you don't think I'm saying this, so I can get something from you. That's not it at all. I just... I wanted you to know."

"I..." I cover his hands with mine and take a deep, shuddering breath. "I have a lot to think about. I'm a little confused. I hope that doesn't sound weird or like I'm brushing you off."

"No, it doesn't. I understand."

My heart threatens to explode when he leans in to place a kiss against my forehead. "It can't be against the rules, can it?" he murmurs with his lips close to my skin.

"I don't think so." But I lean back a little, anyway. "Let's not push it, though."

"That's fair." There's the flash of a smile before he steps back. "I'll shoot you a text when I get in. Thank you for a nice day." There's something so sweet about the way he says it, and for some reason tears fill my eyes. At least they wait until he's already turned away and inside the terminal.

13

HARLOW

He loves me. I mean, that was always a possibility, right? Only a true idiot would tell herself there won't be any feelings attached to a relationship like ours, then actually believe it.

He loves me. I'm almost too overwhelmed to drive home, sort of stuck in a fog. I'm happy, yes, but I'm also troubled. I wish I didn't have to feel this way. I wish I could accept his love happily, openly. There are too many other factors to consider – and people. Not to mention that I never considered falling in love when I got into this arrangement. Sure, it's been months since the breakup with Kyle, but I'm still a little sore, still a little beat-up emotionally. I don't want to rush into anything. And that would be the same if I were in a so-called normal relationship with only Ash.

As usual, my cell is mounted on the dashboard while I'm driving, and when it lights up, my attention goes straight to it. It's Ryder, and he's trying to FaceTime. Interesting.

I answer the call but keep my eyes on the road. "Hi, I'm in the car. Everything okay?"

"No. Everything is not okay."

I stop at a light, giving me the chance to look at him. He's furious, that much is obvious. "What's wrong? What happened?"

"You're seriously going to sit there and pretend you don't know?"

A sick feeling starts trickling its way through my veins, turning my blood to ice. "Why don't you try telling me what's on your mind?"

"You lied to me. Let's start there."

"When did I lie to you?" I'm sitting here going through my memories, trying to figure out what he could be talking about. It might not seem that way since I've done so much lying around the team, but I try to tell the truth whenever possible.

"I got a phone call."

"Okay…" The light turns green and I have no choice but to move ahead, so at least that gives me the excuse of looking away from the phone when he's glaring from it so coldly.

"Somebody disappeared today. Somebody who would've gone to you."

"Why don't you come out and tell me what you're trying to get off your chest? I don't like these riddles."

"Did you know there was a fistfight in a club last night in Seattle?"

I could get whiplash from the sudden change in topic. "Really? Who was fighting?"

"Son of a bitch. Are you driving back from the airport right now?" Of course, he can see what I'm driving past thanks to the angle of the phone. "It's pretty obvious we need to talk."

"I thought that's what we were doing now."

"No. I need to see you, face-to-face." He ends the call before I can ask what he's talking about, and something tells me I'm going to have a guest at the house. With the mood he's in – and how little I feel like dealing with this drama – there's part of me that wants to keep driving once my exit approaches. I even consider it for one brief moment. Letting him sit in front of the house until he figures out I don't appreciate people inviting themselves over without asking.

Especially when it's clear they want to tear me a new one.

But I'm not cruel, and I'm not that petty. Sometimes I wish I could be. Like right now, as I approach my home with a sinking heart thanks to the sight of Ryder's car sitting at the curb.

He can hardly wait until I'm in the driveway, stepping out and slamming his door before I've killed the engine. Before he can say a word, I hold up a hand and shake my head. "No. You are not going to ambush me." Unlike him, I close my door gently before heading for the house.

"He was here, wasn't he? You saw him today."

"I'm assuming you mean Ash?" I can't see him while I'm unlocking the front door, but I hear his groan.

Once we're inside, I toss my purse onto the sofa and spin on my heel, folding my arms and tapping my foot on the floor. "Okay. What is so important that you had to ambush me like this?"

"It was Soren who called me."

"Yeah, I could've guessed that."

"It was him and Ash who got into a fight in the middle of a club." It's clear he's savoring my shocked reaction. "And got thrown out for it."

No. My brain doesn't want to process this. "You're sure?"

"It was Soren who told me about it. Ash flipped out and hit him, and they ended up getting tossed by a couple of bouncers."

The bruise on his cheek. That little liar. It's no surprise that he didn't want to tell me the truth, I guess, even if I wish he had. "Did he say what they were fighting about?"

"That's not the point."

"Then what is the point? Please, enlighten me."

"He was here. He came running to you. Don't pretend he didn't."

"For one thing, why would I pretend? I have nothing to hide."

"Are you sure about that?"

"Yeah, I'm sure about that." I tip my head to the side, looking him up and down. Just when I think he's come a long way and isn't as prone to these outbursts, he surprises me.

"And?"

"And what?" He rolls his eyes and I do the same right back at him. "Nothing happened. God, is this what I've signed on for? Having to explain myself all the time? Last time I checked, you spent the night in my bed – not that long ago, either. If either of them found out about that, I would say the same thing I'm saying to you now. Nothing happened."

"He flew all this way just to, what? Hang out?"

"Newsflash: there's more to me than what's between my legs." I'm not even sure where that came from – but it hit home judging by the way his eyes fly open wide.

"You don't have to tell me that."

"Are you sure?"

"You're not even the problem here. It's him. I don't trust him."

"That sounds like a *you* problem."

"It doesn't help that you kept it a secret. This little visit, I mean."

"It wasn't planned! I woke up this morning to the sound of him at the door. No announcement, no warning, nothing. What was I going to do? Tell him to get back on a plane and get out of here? Come on."

"He did all that, and he didn't tell you about the fight?"

"No, he didn't." And I don't like that he didn't. I don't like it one bit. I would never get in his face and accuse him the way Ryder's accusing me, but I am concerned. He had all the opportunity in the world to confide in me, and he didn't. Why? He's probably ashamed of himself. I would be in his shoes. What are they trying to do? Ruin things for themselves by getting kicked off the Orcas? I could bang their heads together.

And I would include Ryder, too.

"All I'm asking is for a little heads up so I know what's going on. You didn't think to invite me over? Maybe I would've wanted to say hi."

"Don't be ridiculous," I snap. I mean, come on. Could he be more transparent?

"I'm glad you think something that matters to me is ridiculous."

"Stop, please." My head is starting to hurt from all of this. "I need you to listen to me. If this is what I'm in for, I really have to wonder what this is all about."

"What do you mean?"

"I mean I don't deserve this. I don't like having you show up all angry and in my face over something I couldn't control. And we agreed, no sex, or fooling around, or anything unless all three of you are here – but hanging out? Going for breakfast, having a little dinner here at the house? Do you want me to clear that with you, too? That sounds a lot like micromanagement, and I am not going to deal with that."

"That's it? That's all you have to say?"

"Yeah, that is all I have to say, because that's all there is to be said. I'm not going to check in with you over every little thing – and that goes for the other two too. Eventually, you're all going to learn that I am my own person. A grown woman. I make my own plans, I live my own life. And I want you to be a part of it, but I am not going to apologize for something as innocent as what happened today. Got it?"

I can't lie. It feels good to stand up for myself. When I was with Kyle, this would've ended with me apologizing until my voice went hoarse.

He runs a hand over his head and cups the back of his neck, grimacing. "Don't you understand that the secrecy makes it seem like more than it was?"

"I totally understand what you're saying, and I'm telling you, there are other ways to go about this kind of thing than calling me up and picking a fight."

I point toward the door, and my arm is trembling, but I grit my teeth and stiffen my spine. "Now, I'm going to have to ask you to go."

He's hurt. It's clearly written across his face. If there's another thing I got tired of thanks to my years with Kyle, it's managing other people's emotions. I spent years making myself small so he would feel big. I'm never doing that again. Not even for Ryder.

"Fine. I'll go. But maybe you want to think about something." His lips twitch in a smirk. "Why didn't he tell you about the fight? What was he trying to hide?"

"He… was probably embarrassed."

"Probably," he agrees before turning slowly away from me. "But I wonder if there wasn't more to it. Like, I don't know. Maybe they were fighting about you."

A shudder of disgust runs through me, because of course, that's what I'm dreading in the back of my mind. The thought of finding out I was the reason they were fighting, even if I can't imagine why. He's probably planting the idea in my head because he's angry, so I pretend to be unfazed as he saunters to the door. Sometimes, that's the best weapon. Pretending to be unaffected.

When he's gone, though? Once his car pulls down the street and his taillights finally disappear? Then I can sink onto the couch and wrap my arms around myself and wonder what the guys are keeping from me – and why.

14

HARLOW

"Looking good! Don't think about it too much. Let your body do the work."

Don't think about it too much. Easy for her to say. "Just make sure I'm not about to bump into anything!"

"Do you think I wouldn't tell you? Besides, you're in the middle of the ice. There's nothing around you."

Don't think about it too much. Does she have any idea how silly that sounds? It's one thing to be balanced on a pair of thin blades and move without falling. I finally got the hang of it – mostly. I'm still not what anybody would call graceful, but I'm getting better by the day.

Will she let me bask in the glow of my achievement? No way. Now, she wants me to skate backwards.

"That's it. Just move your hips like we talked about. Trust your body. It knows what it's doing."

The worst part is, she's right. It's like when I was learning to ride a bike – something that took much longer than it should have. It seemed like all the kids in the neighborhood picked it up with no problem at all, like one day they didn't know how to ride and the next day, boom, they were racing each other up and down the street and even riding hands-free.

There I was, still too wobbly for Dad to let go without me falling over.

But as soon as I got out of my head and stopped doubting myself, it came easier. Eventually, I realized Dad had let go a half a block back, and it was only my shadow alongside me on the pavement.

Which, of course, is when I fell over. But I got the hang of it eventually.

I'm sure it's the same thing with this. "How do I look?" I ask as I move almost painfully slowly past the point where she is observing my progress.

"Like you're afraid you're going to fall at any second."

"That sounds about right."

"What is the worst that could happen? Honestly."

"Please, don't get me thinking about that. It took long enough for me to heal up last time." Even now, my tailbone will sometimes ache. Like up in Seattle – all that rainy weather left it throbbing. I wonder if I broke it. I guess that's what I get for being too embarrassed to admit I didn't know how to skate. And I'll always have that ache to remind me how useless pride can be.

"Pretty soon, I'll have you doing crossovers," she predicts, then laughs gleefully at what has to be a look of horror on my face. "Relax. I'm not going to make you do it today or even tomorrow. You're fine."

"One thing at a time." It's a relief to come to a stop and hang onto the boards to take a rest. "I hope you don't think you're going to turn me into a great skater overnight."

She makes a big deal of checking her watch, frowning. "No, I think that ship sailed a long time ago. At this rate, I'd be glad to turn you into a just okay skater."

"Thank you so much for your faith in me." We're both laughing by the time we sit down where we left our shoes. As awkward as I still am, I can't pretend there isn't a little bit of pride swelling in my chest. I'm nobody's idea of a pro, but I've come a long way. There's something satisfying about that. It makes me wonder what else I could accomplish that I haven't even considered yet.

"So…" I know as soon as she glances around like she's making sure nobody's listening in that I'm in trouble. "How's it going with you-know-who?"

"Is that what this impromptu lesson was all about?" I hold up my hand to my ear like I'm holding a phone. "Hey, Harlow, my schedule is free this afternoon if you have a little time during your break."

"That's not even how I sound," she grumbles.

"That's exactly how you sounded. Pretending all we were going to do was skate."

"It's not my fault you've been so busy lately – but really, I just wanted to hang out. And hey, you got a nice midday workout out of it."

"Thank you so much." But I can't be mad at her. "And to answer your question, nothing's happening."

"You're kidding."

"No, I'm not." I wish she would take the hint. I really do. It's not bad enough that I'm uncomfortable talking about this in the first place, but it means having to lie to her. Every lie I tell only makes things worse. Eventually, there won't be any coming back from it.

But it's my fault she found out in the first place. I shouldn't have let Ryder sleep over, even if it was innocent.

Especially when I know if I were to do the same thing with Ash, Ryder would throw it in my face.

"So you're not together?" she asks with doubt dripping from her voice.

"Listen." Once my shoes are on, I turn in the seat to look her straight in the eye. "It was inappropriate in the first place. It should never, ever have happened. And that's all I can say. Please, I would rather not talk about it anymore. No offense to you or anything. But it's so touchy."

She sticks her bottom lip out in a parody of a pout. "You don't trust me? Is that what you're saying?"

The thing is, I don't. But then I don't trust Ruby enough to tell her everything about this, either, and Ruby is nowhere near the arena the way Corey always is. She doesn't run into various players throughout her day. There's no chance of her showing up at my front door unannounced with a box of donuts and discovering me in bed with the wrong person. But I still haven't told her, no matter how much I want to. And I've known Corey for, like, two minutes when compared to the amount of time Ruby and I have been friends.

No. It's just too dangerous.

"The less I talk about it, the safer for me," I finally announce with a firm nod. "And that's all there is to it."

"Fair enough. I only want to make sure you're doing okay, anyway."

"I am." Well, that's not exactly true. I'm still furious with Ryder – a couple of days spent without contact hasn't really helped that. The audacity! If anything, spending a little time thinking things over has only made me angrier. The nerve to stand there and judge me. He always jumps to the wrong conclusion. I'm starting to wonder what kind of an opinion he has of me in the first place – though I'm sure if I ever accused him of having a low opinion of me, he'd blame it all on Ash. Like I'm some gullible idiot who needs looking after.

Not for the first time, I notice her checking her phone and biting her lip. "What's up?" I finally ask.

She almost drops her phone, startled. "Nothing. Why?"

"Because your attention is all over the place and it seems like there's somewhere else you need to be."

"No, it's not that." But she doesn't offer any further explanation, either, no matter how long I stare at her expectantly.

"Is there something you don't feel like telling me?"

"It's nothing big. That's why I didn't say anything."

"But…" I wave a hand, gesturing for her to keep going.

"But… I'm going on a date later."

"Really?" I'm surprised. She hasn't mentioned anything about wanting to get back up on the horse or anything like that. Granted, it didn't take me long to get back in the saddle, but Kyle and I weren't engaged, either. We weren't as far along in our relationship as she was in hers. And technically, what happened with Soren and Ash wasn't a date. I didn't think I'd ever see them again.

Her cheeks go pink and she can't stop herself from giggling. "I don't even know why I'm so flustered. I really need to chill out."

"What's his name? What's the story?" I nudge her before she can answer and put on a fake scowl. "Why haven't I heard anything about him before now?"

"Don't get the wrong idea. I met him on one of those dating sites. Hinge. We clicked and he seems really nice. We're just going for coffee, nothing big or involved."

I have to give her credit. She's actively getting out there and trying to find somebody new. "He'll be lucky if you decide he's good enough to go out with again."

She rolls her eyes, but laughs gently. "Maybe I should bring you along. My hype woman."

"Last I checked, I don't have any plans."

"Really, I should get moving. I want to get home and grab a shower." There's a trembling in her voice. Excitement. Considering the absolute mess she was after the break up, seeing her like this is a joy.

"Text me as soon as you get home. I want to hear all about it."

"Yes, Mom."

"You better be careful," I warn as we climb the stairs out of the rink. "Mouth off to your mother like that, and you'll end up grounded. You wouldn't want to miss your date."

15

HARLOW

I f I didn't know better, I would swear it's Christmas morning as I hurry from the car into the building. I don't think I've been this excited about getting to work since the first day I stepped through these doors. It feels like half a lifetime ago, even though it's been less than half a year. I'm starting to feel like I belong. My days have fallen into a pleasant, challenging routine.

Today, though, is anything but routine. Because today, two of our missing team members have returned. Not permanently — there's a chance they'll both be needed again by the Orcas. The option to be called back to Seattle is on the table, and I can imagine it must feel like living in limbo, waiting to see what will happen next.

But for now, they're back. The team is together again. My guys are together again.

Hence the flutter in my stomach as I head to my office and drop my things off. Hence the extra time I took getting ready this morning, like I was preparing for a big date or something. That's sort of what it feels like.

It also feels like it's been too long since I've had everyone together, and I have no doubt that's what tonight will turn into. So yeah, I spent a little extra time in the shower this morning.

I run my trembling hands over my freshly curled hair on my way to the rink. The team is already on the ice, getting put through their paces by the coach. "Come on, let's see some hustle! Just because we're having a good season doesn't mean we get to phone it in at practice!" He notices me and lifts a hand, grinning, but he's surrounded by his assistants and too busy to chat. That's alright. I get the feeling I'd be giggly and flushed anyway, which would probably be a dead giveaway to my excitement. I doubt I could explain it away.

I take a seat, eyes glued to the action on the ice. Everybody seems to be in good spirits, but I'm sure part of that has to do with the way the season's gone so far. There are still bumps in the road, but all in all the team's been playing at a much higher level than

I've watched in films from previous games. And when it comes to mindset, there's sort of a snowball effect. When you're feeling good, you play well, which makes you feel better. It's easy for the guys to have fun, even to joke as they race each other back-and-forth. It's enough to make me smile in relief and maybe a little bit of pride. I know I helped them get to this place. I sort of feel like a proud mother.

Until.

I notice it before Coach Kozak does. The way Ryder checks Ash. The look they give each other. Soren circles them and mutters something — I see his lips move, but of course I can't hear what he's saying from this far away. When Ryder scowls, the heart that was soaring just a moment ago sinks like a rock. Something's wrong.

It could be nothing more serious than a little rivalry. Discomfort. We haven't really gone into it, but I have a sneaking suspicion that Ryder's success in the absence of his teammates left him feeling a little cocky. Like the team didn't need their stars to kick off a winning season. I'm sure the disappointment he already felt when he didn't get called up by the Orcas has played into it. Like even though he wasn't good enough to be offered a two-way contract, he can still lead his team.

No doubt that's part of what's behind the dirty look Ryder shoots Ash before he skates away.

Note to self: get to the bottom of this, fast. Maybe I can cool things down before there's an explosion big enough to alert the Coach and everybody else on the team.

The happy, hopeful rush I've enjoyed all morning is now more like a nagging sense of dread that only gets worse once the coach tells the guys to get in position for a scrimmage game. "I want everybody to go back to the way we had you laid out before the start of the season," Coach calls out with his hands cupped around his mouth. "Let's get comfortable with the lineup." Meaning Ryder, Ash, and Soren are on the same line. My teeth are on edge and my knee keeps bouncing up and down thanks to my strained nerves.

Please, let this go okay. I figured Ryder would be glad to see the guys come back, since it would mean we could spend the night together again. That was pretty shortsighted of me.

This time, when Ryder checks Ash, the coach notices. "Hey! You're on the same team, remember?" He might as well not be talking, since neither of them pay any attention. They're too busy glaring at each other, muttering things I can't hear, but can imagine thanks to their vicious expressions.

And when the gloves come off and the fists start flying, I jump to my feet.

There are shouts of surprise down on the ice, with all other activity coming to a halt once everybody starts watching the fight. Soren is the only one who skates over and tries to break things up while the two of them slam each other against the boards, throwing punches at random. Good. At least he has a cooler head. He'll make a snarky comment and that will break things up.

Or not.

"Stop!" My heartbroken cry is lost in the chaos that erupts when Soren is pulled into the fight, and now all three of them are brawling while the rest of the team tries to break it up. I run down to the bench while the coach skates over to them and puts an end to things, blowing his whistle loud enough to make my ears ring even at a distance. Like magic, the fighting stops.

My stomach turns once I see the damage: Ash has a nasty looking gash over one eye and a bloody lip, while there's already a bruise forming around Ryder's right eye, and Soren now has a bruise on his cheekbone to match the one he gave Ash. They're all flushed, breathing heavy, and there's still obvious anger bubbling between them.

Coach Kozak throws his hands in the air. "What the hell was that? Since when? I don't even want to know who started it. I want all three of you off the ice, now. Go!" He bellows when all three of them stare at him in mute surprise. I'm a little surprised, myself. This is the side of him I've only heard about until now, and I wouldn't want to be the one he's yelling at. Let's just put it that way.

Besides, it's already tough enough being me, standing here and watching the three of them gather their things while the rest of the team looks on, muttering to each other, clearly concerned and surprised. I'm not quite as surprised, but I'm just as concerned. Maybe more so.

"Okay, show's over!" Coach skates over to me, shaking his head. "I've never seen the three of them fight like this. Especially not Soren."

"The guys get into fights sometimes," I remind him. I saw plenty of that in the footage we reviewed together, too.

"But not like that. it seemed... Different. Deliberate. Do you know what I mean?"

I know exactly what he means, and I know he's right. That wasn't a brief dust-up.

"Especially Ash and Ryder," he continues. "They both have those hot blooded temperaments, but what I saw just now… They wanted to hurt each other."

Yes. That's exactly it. He put his finger on what I couldn't quite pinpoint. They wanted to hurt each other.

"Well, to be honest with you…" Because why not start now?

"Please, if you have any ideas, I'm all ears." I feel sorry for the man and all the hope in his eyes. I really do. He's already seen what the team is capable of, and I can imagine it must feel like all of that is slipping away.

"It could have something to do with the two-way contracts. Not to divulge what we went over in sessions, but there might be a little resentment surrounding that."

"Could be." He strokes his jaw, scowling. "I hope that's all it is."

"What else do you think it could be?"

He shakes his head and rolls his eyes. "The only time I've ever seen anybody on this team fight like that, it was over a girl. I hope like hell that's not the case now."

All I can do is stand here and pretend my skin isn't crawling. "Well, I can look into it, see if any of them will talk to me."

"Please do. Because I'm not sure I can handle this on my own."

Of course. I'm probably the reason for the fight in the first place. Might as well see if I can help them work things out.

16

HARLOW

I'm going to wear a hole in the floor if I don't stop pacing, but I have to do something with the nervous energy that has me in its grips. What am I supposed to do? How do I get them through this?

And do I care more about them as players, or as my... whatever they are? Boyfriends? It feels kind of silly, thinking of them that way, but it's as good a descriptor as any.

If only this were as simple as getting them back on the same page so they can play well together. If only life were that uncomplicated. It would be enough of a challenge to wrangle three strong personalities, if I weren't also sleeping with all three of them.

Harlow, how do you manage to get yourself into these situations? Someday, when I have the time, I'm going to sit down and come up with an answer to that question. Right now, all I can do is pace fretfully and wait for Ash to join me in my office. He's the one I want to speak to first. He's the one who wasn't completely honest with me when he came to visit. If I can find out why he and Soren fought, I might start to put the puzzle together. After all, he's sort of the common denominator here. A fight with Soren, a fight with Ryder.

The knock on my door might as well be the explosion of a bomb. That's how my heart leaps, that's how it makes me jump. I hurry to the door and throw it open to find him standing in front of me with an ice pack over his eye and a surly expression twisting his handsome face into a mask of bitterness.

"Get in here," I whisper, stepping aside so he can enter. I barely have the door closed before I practically jump on him. "What the hell was that all about? What are you thinking? Are you trying to get kicked off the team?"

"Since when do we get kicked off the team for a stupid fight?"

"That was more than just a stupid fight, and you know it. It looked like you wanted to take each other's heads off out there."

"Maybe we did."

"But why? Why would you do that?"

He flops down on the sofa and groans. "I don't know."

"Bullshit. You're not being honest with me, and that's the one thing I need from you more than anything right now. Honesty. This is your job we're talking about, and mine. Not to mention theirs. What was the fight all about?"

He heaves a heavy sigh and lowers the ice so I can wince at the sight of the cut just above his eyebrow. "It looks worse than it is," he assures me, though I can't imagine how that's possible. There are two butterfly bandages holding it closed, and already an ugly bruise has formed.

"What is happening?" I ask in a softer voice. "Talk to me."

"I'm just… I don't know. Pissy, I guess."

"But over what? Listen, I know you were having a hard time in Seattle, but you're home now."

"Yeah. Home, sweet home." He looks me up and down and smirks. "Are you asking me all of this as the team's therapist, or as Harlow?"

"Right now, both. You know I care about you, obviously," I whisper. I hate that I have to whisper, hate that I'm always worried someone will overhear. His narrowed eyes tell me he feels the same way. "But I also care about the player in front of me. Either way, I'm concerned. I'm concerned for you."

"Yeah, and you don't need me being an antagonistic asshole." I might not have used those exact words, but now that he has, it sounds about right.

"So tell me. You know you can trust me. I'm here to listen and to help if I can."

"I don't know what to tell you. I really don't."

Finally, I sit on the other side of the sofa. "Does it have anything to do with the fight you got into with Soren up in Seattle? I know that's who gave you that bruise. Why didn't you tell me the truth when you were here?"

His gaze darts away, reminding me of a guilty little boy. "I didn't want you to freak out."

"You knew I'd find out eventually, right?"

"I just wanted that day to be about us. Was that so wrong?"

"No, it wasn't. I understand. But do you understand I'm more worried than ever now? I don't want to see anything come between you guys as teammates or as friends. And I can't help but worry…"

Our eyes meet, and the understanding I find in his tells me I don't have to voice my worries. He understands. "Don't do that to yourself."

"How can I not? Come on. It doesn't take a genius. Was it… about me?" God, this feels so dumb, not to mention egotistical.

"Which fight are you talking about? The one from today, or the one back in Seattle?"

"You're not making me feel much better, you know."

"Sorry. It's… complicated."

"Nope, that didn't help, either."

At least he cracks a smile. "My head's a mess. Maybe Seattle wasn't as great as I was hoping it would be. Maybe I have a lot to think about. And maybe that's getting in the way of my gameplay and the way I act around everybody else." His lips twitch in a smirk. "See? You've got me thinking about my motivation now. Are you proud of me?"

"I'd be prouder if you could vent your feelings in a healthier way."

"I'm a work in progress."

I was so angry with him before he came in. Now, my heart is softening like ice cream left out in the sun. Pretty soon it's going to melt into a big, messy puddle. I know I shouldn't let that happen – I have to maintain some level of professionalism here, but I care about him too much to pretend otherwise.

"I'm going to have to talk to Ryder, too. Just so you know. You guys really got the coach worried out there, and he wants me to get to the bottom of it."

He shifts like he's uncomfortable, which only confirms what I dreaded. This is about me, at least partly. "Is there anything else you want to tell me before I do? Is there anything I need to know?"

"Like what?"

"I don't know. That's the point of me asking you." He's stalling. I don't want to throw it in his face how obvious he is, but he's definitely stalling. Avoiding the question.

"You would need to ask him, I guess. I've told you pretty much everything there is to know on my end. Seattle got me all up in my feelings and I didn't know how to handle it. I still don't."

"We can work through that together, but I need to know you're not going to get into another brawl out there."

"It takes two to brawl." He winces when he touches the ice to his wound. "Sometimes, three." In other words, *I'm not the one who started it.*

Just when I think I have these guys figured out, they go and throw a curveball like this. I feel as lost as I ever have when I get up and he follows me to the door. "Are you going to be okay?" I ask with my hand on the knob.

"What, this? Please. I've been playing hockey my entire life. This is nothing."

"I'm sure that's supposed to make me feel better, but somehow it doesn't."

"Sorry. You really don't need to worry." There's a sudden twinkle in his eye, and he takes a step closer. "Though I'd be lying if I said I wasn't a little bit flattered."

I see exactly what he's going to do before he leans in. "Ash," I whisper, craning my neck to hold myself away from him. "You know we shouldn't."

His face falls but he rebounds quickly enough, shrugging it off. "Hey, it's been a while, and I needed my fix. You can't blame a guy for trying."

"You better get out of here before you have another cut to match the one that's already there." I hold up my clenched fist and arch an eyebrow. "I might not be super athletic, but I know how to throw a punch."

"Message received." At least he's chuckling as he leaves my office. It could be a lot worse. He could be sulking. He has come a long way.

I only hope my meeting with Ryder will go as smoothly. Like Ash said, it takes two to brawl, and it was pretty obvious Ryder had a chip on his shoulder before they even started practice. We still haven't smoothed things over since our last argument, when Ash came to spend the day with me. I hate to imagine that being the reason for the fight, but considering Ash has been out of town all this time, I can't imagine another reason why they'd be at each other's throats.

Now, it's up to me to work things out. Once again, how do I get myself into these situations?

17

RYDER

I'm not proud of myself. She probably won't believe me, but it's true. She's going to ream me out for what happened out there earlier, and I don't blame her. For one thing, it's her job. And for another thing, well, she's supposed to care about us. At least, that's what she says. I want to believe it's true.

But I have to remind myself as I walk down the hall to her office that she reached out as a member of the team, not as my girlfriend. I can't let myself get caught up in our personal connection. I'll only end up more pissed than ever, and I'm already pissed off enough. There's been a chip on my shoulder for days – no, longer than that. But something about Ash's visit has lodged in my chest, burning like a piece of molten steel, searing my insides. It's only gotten worse by the day. No big surprise I wanted to smash his face into the ice earlier.

She's waiting for me, opening the door before I've even lowered my fist after knocking against it. "Just the man I wanted to see." She's not smiling when she says it. "Come in."

"Is that how we're playing this?" I ask as I step into the room.

"What is that supposed to mean? Playing? Do you think this is a game?"

"I'm just saying, are you going to give me a raft of shit? Is this all about the team, or is it about us?"

First, her eyelids flutter. She's surprised, but she recovers and holds up both hands. "Okay, hang on a second. First things first. You are not calling the shots in this meeting. I asked you to come in for an impromptu session. It's pretty obvious there's something going on that's affecting your gameplay."

"Right." I shouldn't snicker, but I can't help it.

"Excuse me." She sits on the edge of her desk, facing me, and even now I can hardly stand having her so close without being able to touch her. I've been stewing in anger for days, but all it takes is having her nearby for all of that to fizzle away into nothing. That's the hold she has over me. That's what she does to me. "I am here to do a job right now. What I saw out there today shook me, and it shook the coaches. Who started the fight? Tell me the truth."

"I did."

Her brows lift, and it's obvious she's surprised before she says a word. "I didn't expect you to blurt it out like that."

"Why not? It's the truth."

"Why would you do that? What did you say?"

"All due respect, but that's between Ash and me."

Her jaw goes tight, but she nods. "Fair enough. You realize you can't do that again, right? I mean, I shouldn't have to say that, but I feel like I have to. You can't go around picking fights, especially not with your own team. I thought you were past all that."

"Do you mean self-sabotage?" Her head bobs up and down. "Yeah, well, sometimes old habits come back."

"But why? What's going on with you? And don't tell me it's all about Ash's visit, because I don't believe it. I feel like you've been holding back for a while now. I can see it in you. Something's bothering you and you don't want to say what it is, but I think what happened out there today is an example of exactly

why you need to get things like this off your chest
before you explode."

The thing is, I know she's right. I wish it were as
easy as she makes it sound to process shit and let go
of it. "No offense, but it's easy for you to sit there
and tell me to work through my shit when you don't
know what's going on in my head."

"For God's sake, tell me, then. As your therapist, as
your friend, as… you know." Right, because she
can't say it out loud. Not here in her office. Just
another thing we have to be careful about.

I can't look at her right now. I am too
uncomfortable. I stare down at my hands, instead,
and the bruised knuckles are a reminder of what I
did to Ash's face, then Sawyer's. I hope she doesn't
expect me to be sorry for that, because I'm not.
Maybe I will be after a little more time to think
things over, but right now it feels too good to regret.

"Be honest with me." There's pain in her voice, and
it's enough to make me look up from my hands. I
don't want to hurt her. It's the last thing I want, ever.
"Was it about me? I hate to even ask that question.
It feels like I'm being an egomaniac. But I have to
know. Am I getting in the way of you guys being
able to play well together?"

"You didn't do anything wrong."

"That's not an answer."

"It's not as simple as that. I don't know, maybe things would be easier if it were. He's obviously got some shit going on, and I didn't like his attitude out there."

"Are you still angry that he came to visit?"

"Did I ever say I was angry?"

"Do me a favor." She folds her arms and rolls her eyes dramatically. "Try that bullshit with somebody who doesn't already know you, okay? Don't waste my time. We both know you were angry – or was that just a joke? It sure didn't seem like it at the time."

"It felt sneaky."

"You thought I was being sneaky?"

"Not you."

"I see." She takes a deep breath before closing her eyes on the release. "I'm getting in the way of your career."

"You aren't. See, you tell me to tell you the truth, and I do, and now you're turning it into a whole big thing. It would be better if we never had this conversation."

"But I need to do my job. See, I'm in a really tough position here. It is my job to make sure you guys get along. I need to be sure you can work your way through problems that come up. And now here I am, one of the problems." She snickers and shakes her head. "Who's the one with a self-sabotage problem? Because I'm starting to wonder about myself."

I could ease her conscience if I told her the full truth, something I haven't gotten the balls to admit yet and probably never will. At least, I don't plan on it.

But why wasn't it me? Why did they get to go, and I didn't? I work just as hard. I'm just as good out there – maybe better, since I'm a hell of a lot more versatile than Ash could be on his best day. I can handle anything the coach throws my way. It's something he's praised me for more times than I can count.

I still wasn't enough for the Orcas to take me. But those two got to go up to Seattle and play with the big boys, and party, and wind up getting into a fistfight in a club, while Harlow waited at home and followed the games and cheered them on. I would never throw that in her face, just like I would never ask her what she thinks they were doing up there as she waited for them here – hell, while I waited for them, too. I couldn't lay a hand on her, but they were partying with fans and getting in trouble. How am I supposed to not resent that?

I could admit it – at least the jealousy part. The feeling of being passed over. I'm sure she would understand, because she's an understanding person with a good heart. I can't force the words out, though. I can't make my mouth form them.

"Don't do that to yourself. If there's shit we need to work out, we'll work it out. But nobody wants you to beat yourself up over it." That much is true.

"Easier said than done."

"Do me a favor and try anyway."

"Then do me a favor and try not to pick any more fights. Please. Do you want to prove you would be an asset in the NHL? Try not starting a brawl in the middle of practice." She taps a finger to her temple. "Am I getting through?"

"Yeah. I get it." When I get up, my hands ache to touch her. Even something as simple as taking her by the shoulders and rubbing them a little so she knows there're no hard feelings on my end. I care about her as much as I ever have. I probably even love her, which makes all of this even more complicated. I love her, and I can't do something as simple as touching or kissing her even innocently.

The way she leans back when I get closer only confirms it. "You know my office is off-limits."

There goes that bitterness again, right on schedule, blooming in the center of my chest and making bile rise in my throat. Her office wasn't always off-limits. I walked in on her getting spit roasted not very long ago, didn't I?

Did you push Ash away? The question is on the tip of my tongue. I bite it back just in time – no matter how satisfying it would be to ask the question, I would feel a hundred times worse if I did. I don't want to hurt her. It's the last thing I'd ever want to do.

So what's the alternative? Hurting them? No, I can't do that, either. I need to figure out some way to work through this – or else everything we've all worked to build together will fall apart.

18

HARLOW

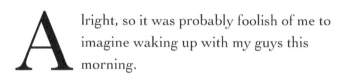lright, so it was probably foolish of me to imagine waking up with my guys this morning.

But it was a natural assumption yesterday at this time. There I was, thinking they would all be so eager for sex after our long dry spell, they wouldn't be able to keep their hands off me. It never occurred to me that they'd get into a huge fight. I sure as hell wasn't about to invite them over after that, especially since I didn't have a chance to talk to Soren about his part in the whole thing, and why he got dragged into the fight when all he was trying to do was break it up. At least, that's how it looked at the time. I could be wrong, but how would I know? He went home before I could track him down. I didn't have it in me to chase after him.

So here I am, opening my eyes in an otherwise empty bed. Certainly not the worst thing in the world, waking up bathed in sunshine and with a day off to look forward to. What's the good of having a day off when all I can think about is work? Because in the end, that's what this is all about. Our personal relationship aside, I have to get them working together if I want to do my job. Not only will it mean making sure they can work together, but it would be nice if one of them didn't randomly blurt out our secret in the middle of a fight.

Even the vague idea makes me cringe and want to throw the blankets over my head, but instead I fling them off before the temptation to lie here and feel sorry for myself gets to be too much to resist.

It looks like a beautiful day, and once I've gone downstairs and stepped outside, I can't help but smile at the rush of fresh air that stirs my hair. It's still only in the sixties according to the weather app on my phone, but I can feel the difference. It'll get warmer as the day goes on, but right now I want to take advantage of the break from the heat. It's been a while since I've pulled my bike out and taken a ride, and if I wear my backpack, I can carry things home from the farmers market easily.

My mind is made up before I've finished my coffee, and soon I'm on my way. My troubled thoughts and heavy heart are no match for the breezy morning, and I can even whistle to myself as I peddle down streets that are still quiet at this time on a Saturday morning. I can almost feel hopeful.

That is, until the conundrum that kept me up late into the night works its way back to the forefront of my thoughts.

What am I going to do about them? Just when I think we've reached a good place, something has to come along and shake everything up. Maybe I'm kidding myself during those good times, pretending like we're on a good course and all of this is a very good idea. No potential for disaster at all.

Yes. I'm definitely kidding myself. The closer I get to all three of them, the better the chances of one or more being resentful and letting that resentment spill over onto the ice.

I can't let this happen, and it's not only because of the danger it would mean for me and my career. I don't want to ruin theirs, either. Sure, they need to learn to get over themselves, but they wouldn't have so much trouble with that if it weren't for me. No matter how I look at this, no matter how long I spend twisting and turning it, I keep coming to the same conclusion. I am the problem. The only way out of this is to take myself out of the equation.

Right away, something aches in my chest at the idea. It's not the first time I've had it — I may or may not have cried myself to sleep last night when I came to that conclusion. I told myself I would sleep on it and give it some more thought today, because in the end, this is the last thing I want. Walking away from them just when things are getting better? After that amazing weekend we spent connecting, having a good time together. I don't want that to end.

But let's face it. It doesn't matter what I want. That's not how life goes. We can make all the wishes in the world, but they don't mean anything. It's time for me to start being realistic and stop letting my feelings guide my actions. I'm supposed to be a responsible adult with letters after my name and all that. I need to start acting like it.

Even if the idea leaves me blinking back disappointed tears as I climb off my bike and start walking it through the market. There are so many smiling, cheerful people around. I wonder if any of them know what it feels like to smile through pain before shaking myself a little. Of course, they do. This particular situation might be unique, but pain isn't unique. We all go through it, and we all have to keep pushing forward. No matter how much it hurts. No matter how much we want to stick our fingers in our ears and yell *la-la-la* like we did when we were kids and we didn't want to acknowledge something.

I doubt any of the guys would be the ones to step up and announce our relationship is over. They're the ones who would stick their fingers in their ears and ignore me, I bet.

Which means I have to be the one to do it. No matter how much it hurts. No matter how much I really, really don't want to. It just doesn't matter. I doubt there's ever going to be a time when they'll be able to share without resentment, or the feeling of being left out. Heck, when I look at it that way, it seems completely unfair to continue with this. I don't want anybody to be hurt for any reason if I can help it.

But this is going to hurt, isn't it? They might not tell me so, but it will. And I'm still going to have to face them every day down at the arena, but I knew that when we started this. I mixed business with pleasure, and there's a reason people say you shouldn't shit where you eat. Why does everybody feel like they're going to be the exception to the rule? Even I did, and I should know better. I've sort of made it my business to learn all the little tricks, all the lies we tell ourselves. What's the old saying? Physician, heal thyself. I guess that wouldn't be a saying if I were the only person who ever had a hard time applying the wisdom they've earned to their own life.

"Smile, pretty lady." I'm surprised when a flower vendor holds out a single, white rose. "For you. You look like you could use something to pick you up."

Normally, I feel the way most women do when they're told to smile, but right now I'm fragile enough and grateful enough for the gesture that I accept the rose with genuine warmth. "Thank you. It's beautiful."

As I continue through the market, I lift it to my nose every once in a while and take a deep breath. It does ease some of the pressure in my head.

I wish it could ease the ache in my chest. I wish it had the power to make any of this easier. But there are some things you just have to push through, some pain you have to experience before it finally eases. This is one of those times.

19

HARLOW

I knew they weren't going to make this easy for me.

I told myself when I asked the three of them to meet me for lunch that they would do everything they could to avoid seeing each other. Granted, they've had to see each other all morning during practice. I made it a point to watch from high up in the stands, and the aggression I witnessed on Friday was nowhere to be found. Coach Kozak happened to look around and spot me watching, and the relieved little smile he wore should've made me feel good. All it did was make me want to shrink away and hide like the liar I am. He thinks I did a good thing, like I talked the guys into getting along. He doesn't have the first clue that I am the reason they were fighting in the first place.

My hands are shaking, and I haven't had a drop of coffee today. I didn't trust myself with it – my stomach is in knots, and I've been fighting nausea all morning, so coffee would only make it worse. My empty stomach growls but I doubt I'll be able to eat a bite until I get this over with. Maybe not even then, depending on the reaction I get. I doubt it's going to be good. I doubt I'm going to come out of this feeling like anything more than a complete monster. No, it wasn't my idea for all of us to be together like this, but I agreed to it, didn't I?

Some things, you just have to go through. Sure, I worried there would be problems down the line. Jealousy, that kind of thing. I hoped they would find a way to get through that for the sake of everybody. But you don't know until you know. I didn't know how volatile their three personalities could be when mixed together. Sure, they're friends, and they get along well when there aren't any big obstacles in the way.

Looks like I am the obstacle big enough to put a wedge between them. I only hope they understand. This is the only solution that can possibly work. I'm sure they'll offer all kinds of promises, but I have to be strong. No matter how much I don't want to.

I haven't even spoken to them yet, mainly because they are being ridiculous and waiting each other out, but I can practically hear their promises already. No matter how much I'm going to want to believe it, I can't break down. No matter how much I don't want to do this, one of us has to be realistic. One of us has to keep our futures in mind, since it's not just about me anymore. They're starting to jeopardize their own careers now, and I can't have that.

It's ten minutes after our supposed one o'clock meet-up when Ryder strolls out like a man without a care in the world. I see straight through him – especially when he pulls up short, clearly surprised to find me sitting alone at one of the picnic benches. He glances around, then scowls. Clearly, he wanted to be the last one to arrive.

"Come on, sit down," I implore.

"I thought this was supposed to be all of us." He thinks he's annoyed with me now? He has no idea what's coming. He barely looks at me before perching on the bench along the other side of the table.

"Are you going to pick up something to eat from one of the trucks?"

He shakes his head. "I'd rather get this over with."

"Okay." He is completely closed off right now. Protecting himself. I hope he can do that, really I do.

I hope he can protect himself from what's about to happen.

It's another few minutes of silent discomfort before Ash joins us, looking about as annoyed as Ryder did when he found me sitting alone. Soren wanders out after another uncomfortable minute. It might look pretty strange, all of us sitting here together without even eating, but then I can always explain it away as a discussion about their fight. Really, that's pretty much what this is about, anyway.

I'm sitting next to Ash, with Ryder and Soren opposite me. It'll be a miracle if I don't get sick all over this table. Now that all three of them are staring at me expectantly, I can't find the words. I don't want to do this. This is the last thing I want to do.

But dammit, it's not my fault. I'm not the one throwing fists in front of the entire team.

It's the memory of their fight that helps break through my dread. I have to do it. There's no other way. "All I ask right now is that you let me get this out before anybody says a word, okay?" Ryder lifts an eyebrow. Soren smirks – big surprise. Only Ash's expression doesn't change. It's almost like he already knows what he's going to hear. I guess it doesn't take a genius, really.

"I think it's pretty obvious there's a problem here." Nobody bothers arguing. At least they give me that much credit. "And it's pretty obvious what it is. I thought this could work – well, I hoped it would. But that's not completely up to me. And now, to see the three of you fighting? Do you understand how difficult that was for me to see? Because I know I'm the reason for it – and don't bother telling me I'm not," I warn when Soren's mouth pops open. "Please. Don't insult my intelligence. I'm sorry if I've come between you. I really don't want it to be this way, truly."

I can't believe I'm about to say this. I take a deep, shaky breath, then decide to tear the Band-Aid off all at once and to get it over with. "I think we need to end this. I think this is where we break up."

"Wait a second." Ryder is going to end up with a sore neck if he doesn't stop shaking his head the way he is. "No. That's not what needs to happen."

"Really? Can you guarantee none of you will let our personal relationship get in the way again? You can't. And I understand. I'm not blaming any of you. I'm blaming myself, if anything."

"You didn't do anything wrong." There's an intensity in Ash's voice that breaks my heart a little. He's barely holding it together, and I want nothing more than to comfort him. But the one thing he wants to hear me say is the one thing I can't say. This is so cruel.

"But I'm not helping, either. And listen, this is affecting my job, too. I'm supposed to be helping you guys improve. Now, I've got Coach Kozak telling me to get to the bottom of your problems. I am the problem. Do you see what that's doing to me, too? I can't keep up with all the lies and excuses, and I certainly can't handle knowing you're fighting over me. I wouldn't be able to handle it even if we didn't work together, but we do, which makes it so much worse. Please, I've given this a lot of thought. And this isn't what I want, I need you to understand that. But it is what needs to happen."

"So that's it? We don't get a say?" Ryder is building up to what could be a pretty big explosion. His eyes are narrowed, his teeth are gritted, and he'll break them if he clenches his jaw much tighter.

"If somebody in a relationship wants to break up, and if they have a good reason, what else is there to say? And this is a good reason. One of us has to be responsible, and if it has to be me, I can handle that. What I cannot handle is watching the three of you flush your potential down the drain because of personal issues. And I can't handle feeling like I'm sabotaging your futures. So that's it. I do still want us to be friends." God, does that sound hollow at a time like this, even though it's very much what I want. "And of course, as usual, I hope we can all keep this between us. It'll be better this way. It'll be easier for all of us. It'll be okay."

Looking at the three of them, it's obvious nothing's ever going to be okay among us ever again.

And there's nothing I can do about it.

20

SOREN

F uck me.

I feel the sunshine beating down. I smell the food being cooked in the trucks behind me, aromas carried on the breeze. I hear birds chirping their heads off like there's something to be happy about.

This is real. It's happening. It's not some nightmare.

But I feel removed from it somehow. I'm here, but I'm not. It's almost like I'm watching a play. Something dark and perverse. And I'm watching myself fighting to keep it together.

Obviously, I knew it had to be something like this. Either we were going to be chastised to hell and back for being naughty boys, or she was going to blame herself for the fight. I suppose it was foolish of me, but I didn't imagine her taking it this far. Sure, there are bound to be bumps along the road, but we work through those. Don't we? Aren't we worth fighting for?

"You know, you've said things like this before." I keep it light, like I'm teasing her a little. It's a habit I fall into easily – maybe too easily. Maybe a lifetime of feeling like I was never quite good enough left me in need of a defense mechanism. I'm sure Harlow would be proud of me for making that assessment, but now isn't the time.

"I know I have." There's a brutal quality to her voice. She doesn't appreciate being reminded. "And that was stupid of me. I need to stop going back on my word. I know this is for the best, no matter how much it sucks."

"Well. At least we know you're not taking it lightly."

She wrinkles her brow when she looks at me, and I wish I hadn't said it. Sometimes, there's no room for sarcasm. What else am I supposed to do, break down crying? Demand she take it back? Right, like that would get me anywhere. "That's mean. You don't have to be mean."

"Don't be an asshole," Ash hisses.

"You can stop kissing ass now," I counter. "She's breaking up with all of us. You included. Or do you think you can get her to change her mind?"

"I have an idea. Why don't you stop talking about me like I'm not here?" She can get good and angry when she feels like it, and she feels like it now. I'm surprised my skin isn't blistering in the heat of her glare.

"I'm sorry," I murmur with a smirk. "But really. We all knew this was a longshot. Making it work, I mean. And we couldn't do it. Oh, well. These things happen."

"Sometimes I really don't understand you," Ash mutters. All Ryder has managed to do is stare at me. I stare back, arching an eyebrow. He looks away first, shaking his head and muttering.

Let them wonder what I'm thinking. Let them ask themselves how I can be so callous. That's a hell of a lot better than letting them witness me losing my shit over this. Not so very deep down inside, that's exactly what I'm doing, but I can't now. None of them can, Harlow included. I am not going to make a fool of myself. Not even for her.

"So that's it?" Her chin quivers and her eyes shine too brightly. Is she going to cry? Dammit, that's not what I want. None of this is what I want.

"Don't get the wrong idea." I would reach across the table and take her hand, but even that could be misconstrued by a witness. Well, they wouldn't be misconstruing, come to think of it. Which would only make things worse. "This isn't how I want to see things go. I don't like the idea of having to break up this way. But what's the use in fighting it? If this is how things have to be, so be it. It would only be a waste of time to do anything else but accept reality."

"Must be easy being you," Ryder mutters, shooting me a filthy look. "You don't feel anything, do you?"

"You're wrong." It takes concerted effort to stay calm. "I feel a lot of things, and I feel them deeply. But I'm a realist, too. And I'm not going to insult Harlow by pretending there's any way to talk her out of this."

"Thank you," she murmurs. I nod my head in response, grinding my teeth against the scream behind them, a scream that wants badly to be heard. This isn't what I want. This isn't how it was supposed to be. I thought I had time, dammit. Time to be with her. Time to tell her how I feel. I never did that, and now I won't have a chance. It wouldn't only be a waste of time. It would be cruel.

If anything, I'm protecting her the only way I can. After all, these two wear their hearts on their sleeves – they look devastated, and if Coach Kozak were to walk past right now, I don't want to imagine the conclusions he'd come to. You don't look as dejected as they do without there being a serious personal issue behind it.

I can at least have a little dignity. Sure, it might sting for her to think I don't care, but it would sting a hell of a lot worse if she knew she's broken three hearts today instead of two.

I feel the weight of Ash's gaze and the resentment behind it. He doesn't get it. I didn't want this. Okay, so I flirted with other women in Seattle, but it meant nothing. Just a little fun, diversion. This is where my heart was. With her, always with her. What was I supposed to do, admit that? I can't even admit to it now, when she's slipping through my fingers.

It wouldn't make any difference. That's what keeps me silent. She's not going to change her mind. And I've never been someone who enjoys banging his head against a brick wall.

Though if she decided to give in and change her mind once I convinced her, damn me to hell, because her future is at stake. When I look at it that way, my petty needs are very small.

That's why I sit here, silently accepting the last thing I want. I doubt I could do it for myself, but I can do it for her.

21

ASH

"So that's it?" I can't wrap my head around this. I just can't.

Soren snorts. "Is your hearing off today? You heard her. But really, it's nobody's fault but our own. We couldn't keep our shit together, and this is what we get."

And he's right. I know he's right. If it hadn't been for us losing our shit, we wouldn't be having this conversation. I took the best thing that's ever happened to me and ruined it.

Doesn't she remember what I said? She won't look at me — and the harder I stare, the more determined she is to avoid looking me in the eye. I told her I love her. Does that mean anything? "Isn't there anything we can do to fix this?" I know what she's going to say, but dammit, I have to try. I'm not going to watch her walk away without at least trying.

"I wish there were. Really, you have no idea how much I wish there were." I'm going to have to call bullshit on that one, because I know what it's like to wish. I'm wishing right now. Wishing I could go back and change things. Wishing I had worked it out with Soren. Wishing there had never been any fight that set all of this in motion. I started that first fight with Soren, didn't I? Why the hell did I let that happen?

I guess in the end, I thought I was protecting what mattered the most. All I was doing was destroying it.

So that's it. I have no choice but to sit here and accept this. I love her, but it doesn't matter. We're over anyway.

I'm shaking when I stand. I can't help it. It's like my body doesn't want to process this any more than my brain – or my heart. "You're making a big mistake." All she does is hang her head. She still won't look at me.

I have to get out of here.

"Ash, hang on!" I keep moving without acknowledging Soren's shouts. I have nothing to say to him now, anyway, and I don't want to hear anything from him. How could I have let this happen?

THIS IS WHAT I NEEDED. I step out of my truck and right away, I fill my lungs with all the fresh mountain air they can hold. Air that's a good thirty degrees cooler than it is down in the valley.

I'm only an hour away from my house, but I might as well be in a different world. Surrounded by towering trees set against a cloudless blue sky. I hear the scratching of small critters nearby and look up to find a hawk circling overhead. "Be careful," I murmur to whatever is nearby. "You probably look like dinner to him."

But that's part of nature, isn't it? Something I had to learn as a kid. Nobody wants to see a tiny, innocent little creature getting snatched up by a predator, but then how does the predator live? That's nature at work. That's the way things have to be, without all our human feelings wrapped up in it.

The sort of feelings I really wish I didn't possess right now, as I begin my hike further up into the mountains near Idlewild. I'm king of the world up here, untouchable — at least, that's what I want to believe. That I'm so far removed from the disaster my personal life has become, it can't touch me. I can't feel it. I can almost imagine being the version of myself I used to be before I met her. I can go back to screwing around, enjoying myself with no strings attached. I can believe that once I get back home, none of this will matter anymore. That I can shake it off the way I'd shake dirt from the treads of my boots.

Maybe the higher altitude is screwing with my head. I don't even know where my thoughts are coming from, like a stream of consciousness gone berserk. That's how I've been all afternoon, ever since that disaster at the picnic tables. I could hardly wait for practice to end before I got the hell out of there, and I've never been so glad that I keep hiking clothes in the truck. I was already planning on coming up here at some point before getting called back up to Seattle.

I didn't expect it to be more like an escape from reality, though. Like a refuge or something.

This isn't like me. I don't roll over and accept things. I don't cower like some pussy, yet here I am. Not cowering, exactly, but it's pretty damn close.

Especially when my phone rings yet again, reminding me of all the phone calls I've ignored. It's more of the same when I pull it out. It was Harlow this time. Last time, it was Soren. Both of them went straight to voicemail.

I haven't had a chance to return the phone to my pocket before it buzzes with a text.

Harlow: Please, don't ignore me. I'm worried about you. At least send me a text back and let me know you're alright.

"Gee, I would, but I'd be lying." There's a sudden rush of blazing heat in my head, and for one moment, I can see myself throwing the phone as hard as I can. I can almost see it's wide arc and the way it would fall. Eventually, the trees would hide it.

Right. Because that would help everything.

She wants to know if I'm alright. What a fucking joke. How kind of her, after she basically spat in my face. I understand why she did what she did, but dammit, she could've pulled me aside. I fucking told her I love her. The first time in my life I've let myself be vulnerable like that, and this is what I get. I get treated like just one of the guys, like there's nothing special about me. About us.

I guess that was the way it was always going to be. She could never afford to give any of us special treatment over the others. What an idiot I've been –

we all have. We told ourselves we wanted things to be a certain way, because that was the only way it would work. Well, it didn't work, did it? Not really. We were all kidding ourselves. Harlow included.

But I went and got my feelings involved anyway, didn't I? I knew better. Somewhere deep inside, I knew this couldn't last forever.

And there's a part of me, a part so big it almost scares me a little, that wants nothing less than forever with her. Talk about being between a rock and a hard place.

By the time I come to a bluff overlooking the valley, I'm breathing hard and sweating a little, even in the cooler air. I take a seat and pull out a water bottle, gulping deeply. There's nothing quite like the sensation of cold water working its way through my overheated body.

My phone starts buzzing again before I've had time to catch my breath. It's Soren this time.

Come on, man. Enough is enough. None of us want it to be this way, but you can't shut us out.

"Oh, yeah? Watch me." Instead of throwing the phone, I put it away with a sigh. Sometimes I wonder about him. I really do. I get that a lot of his attitude is an act. Not that he would ever admit it, but I see it. I've known him long enough to sense when he's saving face. That's the only way I can describe what he was doing earlier. He feels something. I know he does. But he'll be damned before he shows it. He would rather act like I'm being a little bitch.

Maybe that is how I'm acting. Maybe I'm being a little bitch about this. But goddamnit, she means too much to me to pretend I'm okay with this.

I don't think there's anything wrong with needing a little time to myself. I don't think I could face him right now, anyway. He was up there at the club, grinding on some girl who I'm sure he hardly remembers. He's got a hell of a lot of nerve trying to get me to calm down and be reasonable. He needs to spend a little time asking himself if he could've done something to stop this.

Though I doubt he could. I doubt any of us could.

What am I supposed to do now? See her every day and pretend? We were already pretending, and it was already difficult enough. I wonder about her sometimes, too. Is she that naïve? Does she honestly think we can wipe the slate clean and act like nothing ever happened? I wish it were that easy.

But what other choice do I have? It doesn't need to be easy. It just needs to happen.

How did I ever let myself fall so far?

And how am I supposed to tell myself it wasn't worth it, when the short time we've had together was the best time I've ever had in my life?

22

RYDER

Damn. Have my feet always been this heavy? Especially when I'm on my way inside the arena. I always look forward to work. It's what I love to do. An excuse to play and get paid to do it. I mean, what's not to love?

Today, I would rather be doing anything else than what I'm about to do.

I told myself to give it some thought. I spent the night going back-and-forth, arguing with myself. Trying to be sure I wasn't making a huge mistake out of, like, anger or hurt. But now, it's been most of a day since Harlow broke up with us, and I feel the same as I did when I left yesterday.

She did what she felt she had to do? This is what I have to do. I can't see this going any other way.

I'm a good half hour earlier than the rest of the team, but that's on purpose. I need to speak to Coach before everybody else gets here and distracts him. For all I know, he'll lose his shit on me. I don't want them around for that, either. When he decides he wants to be heard, there's nowhere you can go to escape that voice.

I figured I'd find him at his desk, and that's exactly where he is, watching film on his computer. I have to do this. No matter how much it sucks. I tap on the door before I can punk out, and he looks surprised to find me standing here. "Ryder. It's a little early. What's on your mind?"

"I wanted to talk to you privately."

"You did, eh?" He's wary, watching me as I take a seat across from him. "What can I do for you?"

"You can hear me out and not argue with me."

"I don't like the sound of that."

"I'm sorry. I really am. But…" Here goes nothing. "I want to request a trade."

Shit. His eyes go so wide they bulge before he slams back against his chair like he just got hit by a shockwave. His face goes red all at once and for a second or two, I'm afraid I fucked up even worse than I could've predicted. "I didn't mean to shock you."

"Didn't mean to…" His jaw drops before he lets out a long breath. "How was I supposed to react?"

"I'm sorry. I am, really. But I think it's for the best."

"Hold on a minute." He pulls his chair in closer to the desk and sits up straighter. "I was not prepared for that. It is way too early in the day for me to deal with something like this."

"I'm sorry to drop it in your lap all at once."

"Why?" His head tips to the side. "You've been having a great season. You're playing better than I've ever seen you, in fact. Do you feel like you've been mistreated here? Maybe you're not challenged enough?"

"You didn't do anything to push me toward this decision, I swear. You're the best." When that doesn't seem to help anything, I feel like I have to add something. "And what you've done with the team since last season is… Kind of miraculous. Thank you for that."

"What difference does it make if you want to trade out of nowhere?"

"It's complicated." Oh, great choice of words. It's like his eyes literally light up before he leans closer.

"You can tell me, you know. That's what I'm here for. I want you to play well, but I want you to feel comfortable on the team, too. Does it have something to do with the fight? I sensed something happening with you and Ash, and Soren. Is it something I can help with?"

"No." His face pinches a little, probably because I practically shouted it. No, that's the last thing any of us needs. "If it were something you could help with, I would totally tell you about it. But it isn't."

"So it's something that has nothing to do with the game, then."

I knew he would argue, but I didn't expect him to hang on like this. I'm starting to wish I had written him a letter or something just so I could avoid this. All of a sudden, my skin feels like it's too tight for my body. "It's complicated, like I said. It's not easy for me to talk about it."

"Well. I wouldn't want to make you uncomfortable." There it is. I knew surprise would turn to bitterness. I just didn't expect it to happen that soon. Well, I'm sort of screwing him over. I can't blame him for resenting me a little. Finally, he's got his team moving in the right direction, and I'm about to screw everything up.

"Do you think a trade would be possible?"

He scrubs his hands over his face and groans. "Possible? Sure. The way you've been playing this season, there will be plenty of interested owners. I wish you would stick it out here, though. We're finally starting to build something. I hate to say it, but it feels a lot like now that you know what you're capable of, you want to go somewhere else where you can be the star."

"That's not true at all." I wish like hell he wouldn't glare at me the way he is. There I was, telling myself I didn't owe him an explanation beyond what I've already said. I should've known he wouldn't make it that easy.

"So, you're having a great season. You're supposedly happy here. But you want to go."

"Yes. That's right."

"You're going to give up everything you've built here. Your home, your friends."

It's my turn to groan. "Please, believe me. This isn't how I wanted it to be. But there's no other choice."

"Then that answers the question I asked myself after your fight."

"What's that?"

He looks downright disappointed when he shakes his head. "I knew it. I told myself not to read too much into it, but I've seen enough fights to recognize what was in front of me out there. It was obvious what the three of were fighting over."

No. He doesn't know. There's no way he could've kept something like that to himself. Absolutely not.

Right? Or maybe he's been so happy with Harlow's work, he didn't want to fuck things up by calling us out. Shit. Is that it? My palms were already sweaty, but now there's a cold sweat on the back of my neck to go along with it.

"So?" he asks with a sigh. "You're fighting over a girl. It's not the first time that's ever happened. Though I admit, I hoped the three of you were smart enough not to let something like that get in your way."

A girl. He didn't name a specific girl. I'm so relieved, I could laugh.

"Whoever she is, she's not important."

If he only knew. But then, no, he can't ever know. I'm not sure what I should say, either, whether I should argue or tell him he's wrong. I don't know how much I want to engage him or whatever. I mean, I'm not the only one involved here. As pissed as I still am with Soren and Ash, I'm not trying to drag them into this. I'm sure as hell not going to bring Harlow's name into it. I have to protect her. It might be the last thing I can ever do for her, my only way of proving how much I care. She's basically taken all my other options away, after all.

But that doesn't mean I'll stop caring. I wish it were as easy as turning my emotions on and off. I might not feel like I have to do something as extreme as getting the hell out of town.

"Like I said, it's complicated. That's the most I can tell you."

"So you're not fighting over the same girl?"

"No."

"Fine, fine. If it makes you feel better, you can keep it to yourself." He leans back in his chair again. "Obviously, there's nothing I can say to change your mind. All I ask is that you do one favor for me. Just one."

I don't like the sound of this. "I'll do what I can."

"Think about it. Just give it a little time and think about it. Can you do that? Or are you in too big of a hurry to get out of here?"

He will not be satisfied until I give him what he wants, so I offer a shrug. "Fine. I'll think about it. But my decision isn't going to change. I need you to know that."

"Just do me a favor and reconsider, all right? That's all I ask."

"Okay." Not that thinking is going to change anything, but if that's what he needs to hear, so be it. I'll think about it.

And in the meantime, I'll be packing. Because wherever I go, it has to be better than here. Facing her, facing the guys? I don't know how long I'll be able to do it before I reach the end of my rope. I'm not going to let it come to that. I'm going to bow out while I have a little pride left.

No matter how much I wish it didn't have to be this way.

23

HARLOW

The last thing I expected was to be bombarded before I even had the time to put down my purse on reaching my office. My door is still open, giving Coach Kozak the opportunity to storm in. He's not usually like this — normally, he's almost overly careful not to crowd my space.

Then again, he doesn't normally look like he's ready to tear the building down with his bare hands, either. His shoulders rise and fall rapidly with every ragged breath. "Are you sick?" It's the first thing I think to ask because, well, he looks sick.

"No. Not the way you're thinking." I'm still standing next to my desk and gaping at him in shock when he closes the door to give us privacy. "You'll never guess what just landed in my lap."

"What is it?" Countless horrific images race through my head. Does he know? Oh, God, wouldn't that be the cherry on top of the sundae? Here I am, finally doing the right thing, and he found out, anyway.

"One of our players wants to trade."

That doesn't make me feel any better. Especially considering how freaked out he is. He'd be unhappy no matter who was asking for the trade, but this? He looks like he's ready to throw up.

"Which player?" And why do I feel like I should sit down before I get the news?

"Ryder."

No. it isn't happening. Why would he do this? *You idiot. You know exactly why he's doing it.* "I don't understand. Did he…" I can't bring myself to say it.

"What, did he give me the respect of an explanation? No. It's complicated." He makes air quotes around the words before scoffing and shaking his head. "It's not complicated at all, but would he tell me the truth? Of course he wouldn't."

Ryder. I can't believe he feels like he needs to do this. I lower myself into my chair as carefully and casually as I can. Sure, I have to appear concerned, but I can't lose it the way he is. "You think he's lying to you?"

"He's not being honest. I called him out, you know." He grabs the back of one of the chairs across from where I'm sitting so hard, his knuckles stand out bone white. "I told him I know what this is about, but he won't admit it. I swear, some of these kids treat me like I was born yesterday. Do they honestly think they can pull anything over on me?"

You'd be surprised. "What do you think it's about?" Oh, please, don't make me regret asking that question.

"What else? It's about a girl. It's always about a girl." He shakes the chair until the legs scrape the floor and put my teeth on edge. "Everybody thinks they're special. Like they're the first person who ever got mixed up like this. I never had kids of my own, but I'll be damned if I don't understand now why my old man used to lose his temper on me. Because I wouldn't listen. I was dead set on screwing things up."

"That's how we all are," I murmur. I can barely hear my own voice, my heart's pounding so hard. "We have to learn for ourselves. We tell ourselves we'll do things better. Differently. We'll be smarter."

"Yeah, but it always ends up the same, doesn't it?"

Yes, it does. Because I told myself I could handle a relationship even when that was a stupid, selfish belief. Because I was never in this alone, and you can't make somebody get along with someone else. I can only manage myself. I can't force them into anything. You would think somebody with my training would know that.

Who am I kidding? I did know that. But I still put on blinders and told myself we could handle things.

Look where it got me. This poor man looks like he's about to have a stroke. "You should sit down. I mean it," I insist when he rolls his eyes. "Take a breath. Let's talk it out."

"What is there to talk out? He's made up his mind. I got him to agree to think it over for a little while, but that won't last forever." He plops into the chair, then bends to prop his elbows on his knees and lower his face into his palms. "I don't want to do this."

"I know. I would hate to see it happen, too."

"But I don't want him to stick around if he's unhappy, either."

His kindness only drives the knife deeper. I have to practically sit on my hands and bite my tongue off to keep from throwing myself at his feet and begging forgiveness. I was supposed to help the team, not destroy it. I was supposed to get the players working together, not pit them against each other until one of them has to leave.

"Maybe there's some way we can get him to change his mind." Am I being helpful, or am I only making things worse by giving him hope? What's the alternative, though? Telling him there's no use in trying? No, he needs to believe there's a way to stop this, even if there isn't.

And there I was, thinking I had already foreseen every way this could pan out. I went through every outcome I could imagine and always came back to the simple truth that we can't be together.

But I never saw Ryder asking for a trade. Is it that unthinkable, being here after what happened between us? I know how his mind works, and I can only blame myself for not seeing it.

"I'm going to need you to step up for me." He raises his head and his eyes gleam with something close to mania. "You're going to have to get them to work it out."

"Who?"

"Who do you think? Ryder and Ash. It's obvious the problem is between the two of them." He laughs bitterly and shakes his head. "Who do they think they're fooling?"

A rush of adrenaline comes on so fast, I have to fight off a wave of nausea. "Not to argue with you, but

I'm not sure how much I'll be able to do if Ryder isn't willing to come clean."

"But you're the team's therapist. If there's anybody he can confide in, it's you. And I know you've built up trust with all the guys."

"That's true." Good Lord, how much worse can this get? No, scratch that. I don't want to know.

"This is your job, Doc. I'm sorry, I hate to be blunt, but that's how it is. And we both know it."

"Yes, I do know that."

"So you'll talk to him? Both of them?"

What am I supposed to say? "Of course. You can count on me. I'll do my best, but I'm not making any promises."

"That's fine. As long as I know we've attacked this from every angle." I really wish the man didn't have so much faith in me, but there's no helping that now. Already he's seen, in the way the team has turned it around this season, that I know at least a little something about my job. Now, he's desperate for me to bail him out of yet another dilemma.

What a shame it happens to be a dilemma I caused.

"MAYBE HAVING a lesson today wasn't such a good idea."

I lift my brows at Corey, who's watching me with her arms folded and her bottom lip basically disappearing under her teeth. "Why? What did I do wrong?"

"For one thing, I keep trying to talk to you, and it's like you're not even here. Where are you? What's going on in your head?"

"Nothing." I wave my hands and stiffen my spine. "I'm sorry. That's disrespectful."

"You don't have to take it that far."

"No, I'm serious. You're taking the time to give me a lesson, and you deserve my attention. I'm sorry."

"You're forgiven," she teases with a grin. "But I'll be honest with you. If you can't get it together, you're going to end up on your ass – or worse."

I know she's right. I'm clumsy, slow, uncoordinated – even more so than usual. I'm trying to get the hang of skating backward before I move on, but it's like I've regressed from the point I was at just a few days ago. I'm not quite as bad as I was at first, but I'm not that much better, either.

"Why don't you try telling me what's going on, for real." She skates over to me, then taps a finger against the spot between my brows, over the bridge of my nose. "Did you know you get these lines here whenever you're worried about something?"

"I do?" I raise my hand to rub the spot in question, like that's going to help.

"Yeah, and they're deep today. So come on, for real. What's bothering you?"

Tell her. Get it over with. God, I want to. More than ever, I need somebody to talk to. I'm all mixed up and confused and hurt and completely lost. What's the next step? Should I even try to get Ryder to stay? Would it be an insult if I did? Would he even listen to me if I tried? It's all a mixed-up mess in my overwhelmed brain. I could use a sounding board to help straighten it all out.

I only hope she won't judge me for it. I don't want to lose a friend.

"What are you doing later today?"

She lifts a shoulder. "I didn't have any plans. Why?"

"Do you want to go shopping?"

"Sure. But don't you have to —"

"I think I'm going to take a short day." Because honestly, my brain is a hundred miles away anyway. "I think I need a little retail therapy."

"Sure. That sounds good to me." But there's suspicion in her voice, and in the way she looks at me. I don't blame her. I'd be suspicious, too.

She has nothing to worry about. I'm the one with all the problems. And if I'm going to finally fess up and try to get a little advice, it won't be here. The walls have ears.

And something tells me when she reacts, she's not going to be quiet about it.

24

HARLOW

It's a gorgeous day. The sort of day with the power to wipe away even the worst mood. Brilliant sunshine in a sapphire blue sky, plenty of people wandering from store to store — smiling, laughing, talking about the great bargains they just found. I guess that's one of life's universal experiences. Bragging about a great bargain.

"I'm actually sort of glad we came out." Corey bites her lip but can't hold back a wicked little giggle. "I'm starting to wonder if I should invest in some sexy underwear, if you know what I mean."

"Really?" It's sort of nice to have even a brief distraction from my drama. "So things are going well on Hinge?"

"Honestly, better than I thought. I swear, I must have hypnotized myself into buying all of Sean's bullshit for as long as I did. I forgot there are much more interesting fish in the sea."

"I'm really glad. Obviously, we need to get you some fancy things to wear."

"And what about you?" she teases as we enter the store, where we are instantly bombarded by lace and satin and silk in just about every color imaginable.

It wasn't easy to smile in the first place. Now I'm practically breaking my teeth, I'm gritting them so hard. "What about me?"

"Come on. This is me you're talking to." I follow her to a table covered in panties. "I know we haven't known each other for very long, but let's get real. I found you in bed with a hottie not very long ago."

"And I told you, that was totally —"

"I get it. But that's where things start, right? Innocent, friendly. And then they heat up." She lifts her eyebrows suggestively. "So how hot has it gotten? Five out of five flames?"

She needs to change her scale. Things have gotten much hotter than that.

When I don't answer right away, she stops sifting through piles of satin and turns her full attention to me. "Hey. Is that what's going on? Are you having problems with him? I swear, I meant it when I said your secret is safe with me. You can tell me anything. I owe you that much, at least."

I just have to get it out. I have to say it and be done with it. I was wrong, thinking I could ever keep this to myself and not totally lose my marbles.

"Things have been extremely complicated."

"Because of your job?" she whispers with her brows drawn together like she's in pain. "I'm sorry."

"It's a little more than that."

"Really?" She's trying to hold back her ravenous interest, at least. I'll give her credit for that.

I crook my finger, gesturing for her to follow me to a rack in the back corner of the shop. There aren't a ton of people around in the afternoon in the middle of the week, but still. This isn't the kind of thing you blurt out in the open. People tend to judge.

I only hope she doesn't.

I can't believe I'm about to spill my guts next to a rack of bra and panty sets. "So listen. I really hope you don't think any less of me because of this, but I have to tell somebody. I've been going out of my skull, keeping this to myself all this time."

"What is it? Are you…" She gives my belly a pointed look that needs no explanation.

"No, it's not that. But… things have gotten really complicated in my personal life. I know it's wrong. I know I never should've gotten started with it. But I couldn't help it. I tried, I really did."

Her playful grin slides away. "Harlow. What are you trying to tell me? It can't be that bad, can it?" She's starting to sound like she wishes I never started speaking.

"I have been seeing Ryder."

"I knew it."

"But not only Ryder." Here goes nothing. "I've been seeing two of the other players, too. Soren and Ash."

Her head snaps back a little. "Wait. What? You've been dating three players? Do they know about each other?"

"They know. Because…" I can't look at her anymore. Not when she's so concerned and confused. Instead, I examine the embroidery on a sheer bra dotted with pink and white flowers. "Because I've been seeing all of them at the same time. Like, all at once."

"Seeing them... all at once..." She can't stifle a gasp while gripping the metal rack like she's trying to keep herself on her feet. "Like... a gangbang?"

"It wasn't like that. Seriously, it wasn't."

Her eyelids flutter, and she sort of sways a little before catching herself. "I need a minute." My heart sinks when she turns away and heads for the door. Dammit. I should've known. No, I did know. I knew this wasn't the kind of thing even a sweet, supportive friend like Corey would understand.

She goes to the nearest bench and sits down with her hands clasped between her knees. I'm almost afraid to approach, so I take my time instead of rushing her. I knew I'd get a reaction like this, didn't I? That's why I never said anything. "I'm sorry if I shocked you," I murmur once I'm close enough for her to hear me.

"I'm sorry if... I made you feel bad." She blows out a heavy sigh and stares at the ground. "It's just a lot to wrap my head around. I'm not judging you, I'm really not. But this sort of goes against who I thought you are, you know?"

"You mean, the sort of person who doesn't get involved with three men the same time?"

"Not just three men. Three men you work with."

I sit on the bench with a sigh of my own. "I know. I wish I could explain."

"You don't have to. That's the one thing you do not have to do. I'm not asking for an explanation."

"I know. But I still feel like I need to have one."

"It does sort of worry me for your job."

"Well, you don't have to worry about that, because I broke it off. For good. I mean, the guys are out there fighting on the ice in front of everybody, and I know it's because of me. Or at least, I'm part of it. I needed to take myself out of it before things got worse, and the wrong people heard the wrong things."

All at once, emotion lodges itself in my throat. I wasn't planning on breaking down and blubbering like a baby. Then again, nobody plans on that kind of thing, I guess.

No matter how I try, I can't blink back the tears that insist on filling my eyes. "But now, everything is so much worse."

"What do you mean?"

"Ryder wants a trade." I'm impatient as I wipe away the tears that have overflowed onto my cheeks. "The coach came in and told me today."

"Oh, no!"

"And now, Coach wants me to find out why, but I know why. I know it's because he thinks it will be easier to go away. But I don't want him to go away, and I hate thinking I affected the team like this. Just when they were doing so well, too."

"Back up for a second." The hand she places against my back is gentle. Understanding. "Yeah, you have the team to worry about, but it's okay to worry about yourself, too. You're going through a pretty complicated situation. You're allowed to feel how you feel."

"This is all my fault. That's how I feel." I can't hold it together anymore. I cover my face with my hands, shaking like a leaf as guilt and regret roll through me. "I thought I would make things easier and better by breaking up."

"Did you really want to do it?"

"No. I didn't want to. I mean, I knew I had to." I wipe away my tears, though it's a lost cause. I can't keep up with them.

"Do you wish you hadn't?"

"Maybe none of this would be happening if I never broke it off."

"And maybe it would."

She has a point. But… "I'd still be with them. You know? Now I'm miserable and guilty and alone."

"You did what you thought had to be done. Don't blame yourself." She snickers softly and starts rubbing my back the way I rubbed hers when she was in the grips of despair not so long ago. "You have three other personalities involved in this. You weren't in it alone. You couldn't predict what they would do. And men like to call us emotional, right?"

"I know. It's ridiculous."

"Do you think Ryder will even want to talk about why he decided to leave?"

"I honestly don't know." I only know the coach expects me to make everything okay, and I don't know if there's any way that's possible.

25

SOREN

I didn't understand until now, standing in the middle of a crowded club, that I never expected to do this again.

I mean, I did it back in Seattle. That was innocent enough. I was never going to hook up with any of the girls up there. Not when I couldn't stop thinking about Harlow. Missing her, wanting her, wondering how she was. I never intended to pick up another girl in a bar or a club or anywhere, ever again.

And that was wrong, anyway. Harlow was never going to be mine. Not mine alone. There was never going to be a forever for us.

The cute blond who keeps looking my way over her shoulder does it again, and this time she sinks her teeth into her plump bottom lip when she catches my eye. She might as well be holding up a sign saying Open For Business.

We're over now. Harlow, all of us. It's in the past, it's history. And somewhere deep down inside, I know that was for the best. Being together would be complicated enough without bringing the team into it.

So why does it feel so much like I'm cheating as I approach the girl with the big tits and the welcoming smile? I have to shake off the feeling as I elbow my way through the crowd.

"It's about time." She grins up at me, and the smell of the perfume and hairspray and whatever else she's using is almost overwhelming. But then there are a lot of people around us. A lot of conflicting scents. Everybody's trying to attract somebody else.

"About time for what?"

"About time you finally came over here to talk to me. I've been waiting for you."

"I'm honored."

"You should be."

I like her style. It's easier to relax a little. "What's your name?" I ask, holding up a hand to get the bartender's attention.

"Steph. What's yours?"

"Soren."

Her head tips to the side the way I expected it to. "Where are you from with a name like that?"

"I've been living here, in California, for a long time. But my family lives in the Netherlands."

"Oh, cool. So why did you come over here? It's supposed to be so nice over there."

She's right about that. It is nice. Beautiful. An entirely different way of life. There are still things about this country I can't understand. "I wanted to get out of the family business."

"That sounds mysterious."

"It isn't, very." She doesn't have to know the finer details. Nobody's trying to open up and tell their life story in a situation like this. She's hot, and she's smart and intriguing, but we both know what this is about. I need someplace warm and wet to stick my dick.

That's why I don't bother telling her about the way I grew up. The way my father would've rather that I do just about anything else than play professional sports. How he expected me to follow in his footsteps the way he followed in his father's. The standards I was expected to uphold. The family name I couldn't tarnish.

Family. As if any of them really understands what family means. Hell, the closest I've ever had to a real family is my team. We might be fucked up, we might fight and compete and even hate each other sometimes, but it's a hell of a lot more functional than what I left behind when I got on the plane without looking back.

Shake it off. This isn't the time to get depressed or brood over things I can't change. I'm supposed to be having fun. It doesn't come naturally to me — one thing nobody else really knows. Not even Ash, and I've shared more with him than I have with anyone. This attitude I put on. Trying to be carefree, trying to keep things light… That's not me. It's who I have to be if I want to fit in around here, in this country. Everyone is so friendly and open. That's one way they do it better over here, for sure.

"Are you okay?"

I look down to find her frowning. "Sure. Don't I look it?" I make a big deal of checking out my outfit, that sort of thing.

"That's not what I meant. You looked kind of unhappy." The hand she places against my chest is light, teasing, but not unwelcome. "What can I do to put a smile on your face?"

That little question alone is enough to get my engine revving. Not just the question, but the way she asks it. There's no need to wonder what's behind her coy, playful tone. "I can think of a few things."

"So can I." She taps her nails against me, smirking. "But I could use a drink first."

Finally, the bartender approaches, and I order for both of us. I wonder if a girl like this — beautiful, clever, sexy — would one day end up turning into a woman like my mother. Was she ever like this? She must have been to some degree, at least, or else she never would have fooled my father into thinking she was worth marrying. I wonder how long it took before she let the mask fall, since all she was ever interested in was his money. I know that much. That's still all that interests her, spending his wealth. I can count on one hand the number of Christmases we spent together, the years she wasn't off with friends in one fabulous place or another. Sometimes she wouldn't even call, and later I would get an excuse about her losing track of time. As if Christmas day doesn't fall on the same date every year.

"What do you do for a living?"

Yes, that question usually comes up. "I play hockey."

Her eyes go wide on cue. "Like, professionally?"

"Yeah. Not in the NHL, though – but I was up in Seattle for a while, playing with the Orcas. I might end up back there this season."

Her interest just went from high to extreme. What is it about athletes that turns women on so much? I mean, not that I would ever complain. I've definitely used it to my advantage many times. And I'm going to use it to my advantage again tonight. I know I will. That's the entire reason I came out at all.

Even if it feels like I'm going through the motions, just like I go through the motions of being who I need to be. The sort of social skill Ash possesses has never come naturally to me, which is why I compensate so hard for the lack of it. I doubt I'll ever feel quite at home here, no matter how much I wish I did.

In fact, as I stand here sipping on whiskey while the girl whose name I've already forgotten drinks a martini, it hits me that the only time I can remember feeling really plugged in and alive, like I really belonged, was with Harlow. That last weekend we spent at the lake, the four of us. I was me, really, and truly. Relaxed, at ease. At peace with the world and with life.

Compared to that, making small talk in some generic club falls pretty damn short.

But I have to forget her somehow, don't I? If not forget, then at least get her out of my system. I'm too damn young to spend the rest of my life longing for a woman who either doesn't want me or doesn't consider being with me worth working for. No matter the reason why, the outcome is the same.

The blond — was it Stacy? Sarah? — polishes off her colorful drink before giving me a playful little smile. "What do you like to do for fun, Mr. Hockey Player?"

My dick responds in the usual way, but I still have to force a smile. This is so fucking empty. Am I always going to feel this way? Has being with Harlow ruined me for every other woman for the rest of my life?

I bolt back what's left in my glass, feeling a little grim but determined to push past it. "How about we get out of here and I'll show you?"

26

RYDER

All I want to do today is stay in bed and pretend the world doesn't exist for a while. At least, that's the plan. I'm used to getting up early, even on the weekends, even when I don't want to — one of those things your body trains itself into. Plus, I've always read it's no good to fuck with your schedule on the weekend the way most people like to do. It throws off your natural rhythm or some shit like that.

This morning, I don't give a damn about my natural rhythm. I don't care about very much at all, really. Not even the decision I'm supposed to be rethinking to make Coach Kozak happy. I mean, I told the guy what he needed to hear, but I'm not changing my mind. I doubt anything could make me do that. Anything reasonably realistic, anyway.

I mean, Harlow's not coming back. That's over. And I doubt facing those two will get any easier even with plenty of time to smooth things over. Hell, they'll probably go back up to Seattle any day now, so it's not like we could have much of a chance to work things out, anyway.

With my luck, I'll stick around, and they'll never go back, so I'll have to see them all the time. No, that doesn't seem like it would be any easier. This is a shit situation all around, no matter how I look at it.

The last thing I feel like dealing with is my ringing phone. It can't be too early — the birds have been singing for what feels like forever, and I've been fighting to keep my eyes closed in spite of the sunlight shining on the other side of my eyelids for what feels like just as long. Still, not many people in my life actually bother calling, not when it's so much easier to send a text. Especially on a weekend morning when people don't usually want to be interrupted.

It's a relief when the noise stops — but then it starts back up again right away.

Of all times for Harlow's face to flash in front of my mind's eye. What if something's wrong with her? What if?

It's not her or anybody else from the team. "Erin?" I whisper, and now I'm torn between whether I should ignore the call from my foster mother or find out what she wants. It's not that we have a bad relationship or anything like that. But it's not like there was ever any affection. I was too old for that by the time I landed on her doorstep. I had been bounced from too many foster homes by then. Letting myself get attached was a liability, and I didn't want to put myself through that again. I'm sure it couldn't have been easy for her to deal with my sullen ass.

That's what makes me answer the call. Remembering how she always tried.

"Hello? Erin?"

"Ryder. Thank God you answered. I don't know what I would've done."

I sit upright all at once. "What is it? What happened?"

She answers with the two words I was dreading. "It's Pete."

I squeeze my eyes shut and rub the bridge of my nose. "What happened this time?"

"He got kicked out of school, and he's damn lucky the other kid's parents didn't press charges."

I remember being seventeen. Your body is basically going through hell every single day, hormones raging, no idea what to do with the feelings and the random anger that springs up sometimes. At least, it did for me. Considering Pete's life has been a lot like mine was, it wouldn't surprise me that he's battling the same shit I did. Always feeling like he's on the outside, looking in. Like everybody else gets to live a normal life with a normal family, but not him. We have too much in common for me to react with anything but sadness. Anger might come up later, but not yet.

"Where is he? You need me to talk to him?" Sometimes, that's all that will get through to him. Talking to me. It's kind of a big responsibility, but he is the only family I've got, even if we aren't related by blood.

"You'll be talking to him when you pick him up at the airport."

"When I what?" I snap. "What are you telling me?"

"I did the only thing I could think to do, Ryder. I'm sorry, but sometimes these are the choices we need to make. I put him on a plane first thing this morning. I've been trying to get a hold of you ever since, but of course —"

"The time difference." I check the time now and find that it's past nine. "Shit. When does he land?"

"Ten-thirty your time."

"I don't know what you want me to do."

"Being out here is no good for him, Ryder. You had hockey. He has nothing to take his mind off things. It's difficult for him to make friends. He doesn't want to talk to anybody around the house. You're the only person he's ever trusted and respected and listened to."

I know she's right, but that doesn't make it any easier to wrap my mind around this. What the hell am I supposed to do with a seventeen-year-old?

I'm still asking myself that question on the way to the Palm Springs airport. I should get there in time to pick him up without giving him the chance to wander around too much. Not like I can't trust him to handle himself in an airport, but still. The kid's never been on a plane by himself in his life, and he's never been out here. It's a whole different world. I should know, after all.

I barely recognize the tall, skinny kid waiting at the baggage claim. His profile is the same, though, and so is the sandy blond hair that could use a cut. He even stands like he's got a grudge against the world, but I know the truth. He's scared shitless. Again, I should know.

"Yo, asshole." I give him a shove from behind and he whirls on me before letting out a relieved sigh. He then gives me one of those awkward half hugs guys give each other all the time.

"I'm sorry about this. It wasn't my idea."

"Don't worry about it. Let's just get your bags and I'll take you home." But it isn't home. Not for him. Hell, I wasn't even planning on it being my home for much longer. I was ready to pack the place up and move on, and now I've got a teenager to take care of.

"Wow. It's so warm." His head swings back-and-forth once we're outside the airport on the way back to the car. "Is it like this all the time?"

"It's hot as hell in summer, but this is nice. Better than Boston, I guess."

"Yeah, it was freezing when I got on the plane." He laughs softly as I drop his single bag into the trunk. That's all he brought with him. "Isn't it crazy how you can get on a plane and end up in a different world?"

"What put you on the plane? What happened?"

"I don't want to talk about it." He gets in the car and closes the door harder than he needs to, which sets my teeth on edge. Of all times for this to happen. I'm not exactly feeling patient.

Once I'm behind the wheel, I ask again. "What happened? You're out here with me now. I think I deserve to know why."

"The same old shit. These assholes at school, always talking shit. I told the prick to keep his mouth shut, but he didn't want to. So I shut it for him."

"How?"

"I kicked his ass, that's how. What do you think? He needed stitches and everything."

"I know you don't sound proud of what you did. I know that's not what I'm hearing, right?"

"I don't know what you want me to say."

"How about we start with you promising not to do anything like that again?"

"Well, it's real easy to promise when you're not facing down two or three assholes saying shit about you. You know?"

I do know. That's the thing. That's what makes me feel like a huge hypocrite. I have no business tearing him a new one when I would've done the same thing. Hell, I did pretty recently, didn't I? Right in front of the whole team.

"Listen. What happened back there is what happened back there. When you're out here with me, I need you to knock that shit off. You got it? No fighting, no getting into trouble. You're going to be on your best behavior. Got it?"

"Got it," he mumbles. The sound of it softens me up a little. He's still just a kid, and he just got shoved onto a plane so somebody else can handle him. I know when I was his age, what I needed more than anything was to feel like somebody cared.

"I guess it won't be a surprise when I tell you I'm not really set up for a long-term guest. We can stop over at Target, pick up some sheets and whatever clothes you need. Whatever it is, you've got it." I slap his leg with the back of my hand. "And then we can go for some In-N-Out Burger."

"I am starving," he admits with the beginnings of a grin.

"Maybe we'll do that first. It's a little early, but it's sort of a special occasion, right?"

I'm nobody's idea of an ideal parental figure, but then I don't have much of a choice, do I?

27

RYDER

With our stomachs full, we head into the store. I grab a cart while my head spins. I still can't get used to this idea. No, it's not going to be forever. It can't be. I'm not raising this kid, even if he is almost eighteen and not a child anymore. It still feels the same, like I have to provide for all of his needs and give him guidance and all sorts of stuff I'm not prepared for.

"So, what did you bring?" There couldn't have been much room in the duffel bag still in my trunk.

"A few things. Just some clothes."

Now isn't the time to get resentful about the way this is all playing out. Erin assumed I would take care of all of his needs once he got here. I guess it's one less thing for her to worry about.

"No problem. I've got you covered." Because none of this is his fault. Well, maybe the trouble he got in, since he's the one who decided to get physical with the kid. But otherwise, life handed him a shitty hand from the beginning. He's doing the best he can to get through it.

"You really have this kind of money?" he asks once we're in the bedding section and I grab a few sheet sets for the double bed in the guest room. I've never had a reason to get the room set up beyond the very basics. No guests.

"I get paid well."

"Shit. Maybe I should've started playing hockey when I was younger."

"It's not like you're free to print your own cash or whatever." I'm starting to think I should've gotten a cart for him, too, since next we have to head to the men's department and buy him some clothes. I guess not everything has to be picked up right away. We could come back another day for the rest of it.

What am I supposed to do with him? What's he going to do during the day while I'm at the arena? Letting him hang around the house and do nothing isn't exactly a plan. The more free time he has, the more chance he will get into trouble.

"I don't need all that much." It's like he's reading my mind as he stares down a wall of folded jeans in all sizes and styles. "Just a couple pairs of pants, a few t-shirts."

"You need more than that." All he does is frown at the wall of denim. "You deserve more than the basics," I tell him in a quieter voice. That's the thing about growing up the way we did. It wasn't all bad, but when you've bounced from one house to another from a young age, and it seems like nobody actually wants you long-term, you sort of get the idea about yourself that you're not worth much of anything. At least, I did. I'm thinking he did, too.

It takes a little time, but he starts getting into it. "Grab some sweatshirts, too. It's warmer here, but it gets colder at night." I have to make sure he picks up socks and even underwear, because he's still a teenage boy who doesn't think about things like that.

Next is the shoe department, since the sneakers he's wearing look like they're about to fall to pieces before we even leave the store. "This is too much," he decides after finding a pair that fits well.

"No, it's not. What did I just say? You deserve more than the minimum."

"Shit, at this rate, I'll need to buy a big suitcase to pack everything up when I go back." His voice fails a little, though, and he sort of trails off. He's uncertain again, the way I am. When will he go back? What will he be returning to? He'll age out of the system before much longer.

The situation is starting to look more enormous every minute we spend together.

All I can do is focus on right now. Today, maybe tomorrow. If I try to look at the whole mess at once, I'll go out of my mind. I guess there's a reason people in recovery are supposed to take things one day at a time.

Our last stop is the toiletry section, which spans aisle after aisle. He seems fairly clueless on what to get beyond body wash, so I talk him through the finer points of grooming as I add items to the cart. It's so heavy, I'm surprised I can still push it. "You need razors. Shaving cream." I study his skin for a moment and am glad to see it's smooth and clear. "We can keep it simple."

"What, do you do a skin care routine or something? Is that what living in California has done to you?"

"Hey. Gotta look good for the fans." He laughs, but I feel hollow inside. I don't give a shit about the fans — not that way, not anymore.

I'm starting to think Pete couldn't have come along at a better time, since at least I'll have something else to think about now.

We round the end of the aisle so he can find a toothbrush, and at first, it takes a second for me to recognize who's picking up floss and toothpaste only a few feet ahead of me.

Her eyes fly open wide when she sees me standing behind the cart while Pete chooses a toothbrush at random and tosses it on top of the pile. He gives me a funny look, but I guess I look funnier than he does. I'm probably staring with my mouth hanging open, and every lonely, longing thought that weighs on my heart must be written across my face.

"Hey," I murmur, because that's the coolest thing I could come up with.

"Hi." Harlow looks at the cart, then at Pete, then at me.

Right. I've never talked about him. "Harlow, this is Pete. He's my foster brother from back in Boston, and he'll be staying with me for a while."

"Oh!" She extends a hand, wearing a brilliant smile I wish would shine my way. "Harlow Jacobs. It's nice to meet you."

"Same here." Yeah, he's checking her out. I can't blame him. I've been checking her out since the minute I set eyes on her. She's dressed like she just came back from a workout, wearing leggings and a zipped up hoodie. Of all times for us to run into each other.

"Pete just got into town," I explain, even though she didn't ask. "I needed to get him set up at the house."

"I see. Well, Pete, welcome to California. Hopefully, we'll run into each other again." She's warm, cordial, but I see through it. This is just as awkward for her as it is for me. I can't look at her without having to fight the impulse to take her in my arms.

Once she's around the corner, Pete slowly turns my way. "Who was that?"

"I told you. Her name is Harlow."

"You know what I mean. Who is she to you?"

There's a story he does not ever need to hear. but I can't tell him she's nobody, either. It was pretty obvious from that awkward exchange that there's something going on.

I decide to keep it simple, since even talking about her involvement with the team could be complicated. And I sure as hell would never bring Soren or Ash into it. "We dated for a little while, and the breakup wasn't that long ago. So it's still a little fresh."

"You dated her?" The way he stares at me, it's pretty clear he doesn't believe it.

"Yeah, and I hope one day to get the hump removed from my back."

"No, no, I'm not saying you're ugly or whatever. But she is…"

"Out of my league. I know. You don't have to tell me."

He snorts gently as we head to the registers so I can see what all of this is going to cost me. "She must be smart, since she figured it out and dumped your ass."

No comment.

28

ASH

"Come on! Keep your head in the game!"

If I had a dollar for every time Soren shouted that at me during this game, I could retire easily. At least that's how it feels. It also feels like my brain and my body are completely disconnected. No matter how I try, I can't get into a good rhythm. It's like I just laced my first pair of skates this morning. Weeks ago, I was up in Seattle playing with the big boys. Now, I can't even handle a minor-league game against the Rattlesnakes.

It's like living through a nightmare. I used to have dreams like this when I was a kid, like I'd show up at school for a test I never studied for, or I was called up to speak in front of a bunch of people when I had nothing planned. That kind of thing. Right now, I'm dreaming I'm supposed to be a professional hockey player, and I somehow forgot everything I thought I knew about how to play. Pathetic, but painfully true.

Focus. You know what you're doing. I know I'm supposed to talk myself out of it, be positive, and all that, but at the moment I just feel like I'm lying to myself. That only makes everything worse.

I'm screwing up. I'm ruining this. I'm ruining everything.

One of the Rattlesnakes glides past, and he doesn't bother pretending he isn't amused by the way this is going. "What happened, you forget how to play when you were out of town?"

"Is that the best you can do, Anderson?" Ryder appears at my side out of nowhere, and he's glaring at the trash talker. "Your defense isn't the only thing you need to work on."

Then he turns to me, and I hate what I see in his eyes. There's concern, sure, but it's more than that. It's a pity. I hate him for that.

"Don't let it get to you," he tells me. "Just try to have fun, yeah? Remember why you're playing."

That's the thing. Right now, I can't remember. Why do I do this? What was the point in the first place? I used to love this, didn't I? I feel like I did. That's what my memory tells me. Right now, I'll be damned if I know why. What the hell is happening to me?

There's no time to think it over with the game moving as fast as it does. I skate until my legs burn, moving as fast as I can, but I'm still clunky and distracted when the puck comes my way. I am barely able to take the pass and get control of the puck while scanning the area, looking for a clear lane.

I pass it off to Danny, and right on time, since the next thing I know I'm slammed against the boards hard enough to make my ears ring. Everything around me goes a little fuzzy for a second and I shake my head to clear the cobwebs.

It was the same trash talking dickbag as before, and he's now grinning over his shoulder as he skates away. Asshole.

I can barely breathe for the tightness in my chest. Who the hell does he think he is? Who does he think he's dealing with? I'm flying up behind him before I know what I'm doing, and a sharp shove makes him stumble and almost fall.

"Oops!" I shout when he whirls on me. "It sucks getting blindsided like that, doesn't it?"

"What, are you going to be a fucking crybaby now?" he shouts.

"You should watch the shit that comes out of your mouth if you don't want to end up spitting out your teeth."

"Is that supposed to be a threat?"

I don't answer in words. My answer comes in the form of a dropped pair of gloves and a punch to his jaw. Something inside me roars in approval even though deep down inside I know I'm fucking myself by doing this. It feels too damn good to vent my frustration on this prick, even after we're pulled off each other and I'm sent to the penalty box for five minutes.

It's no surprise when Coach practically pounces on me. "What the hell do you think you're doing out there?" he screams in my ear. "Since when do you pull shit like this? Who are you?"

He doesn't expect an answer – it's definitely a rhetorical question. Good thing, because I wouldn't know what to say if I tried. I don't know why any of this is happening. I don't know who I am anymore. I don't even know why I'm here. If I can't handle being down a couple of goals, if I can't let trash talk roll off my back, what business do I have wearing this jersey?

He finally gives up and goes back to yelling at the rest of the team instead of focusing on me. I have to sit and watch while the Rattlesnakes score yet another goal on us. At least I can't blame that one on myself, since I still have a couple of minutes before I'm allowed back on the ice.

She's watching. I don't know where she is, but I know she's here. She's watching me make a goddamn fool of myself. I can't shake the feeling of trying to hold onto something as tight as I can, and watching it slip through my fingers anyway. I'm watching what could end up being my future slip away from me, and I've never felt so helpless in my life. This isn't me. I don't roll over and play dead when there's a challenge or an obstacle in my way. Yet here I sit, fighting the feeling that I am losing everything that used to be mine.

It's that feeling that propels me back onto the ice once five minutes is up. It's anger that pushes me, that forces me to push myself. Somebody has got to turn this game around.

And it's not going to be me. "Fuck!" My scream is drowned out by the buzzer signaling yet another goal for the Rattlesnakes.

My heart is about to race its way right out of my chest. I can barely breathe. Something like panic spreads its way through me, and I've never in my life felt this stuck. I'm unable to do what I have to do to help my team.

So when I spot the asshole with the big mouth, I go out of my way to bump him on my way past.

And I'm so busy hating myself and questioning why I'm here that I don't notice when he lowers his stick in front of my feet. One second, I'm on my blades. The next, I'm tripping, I'm falling, and the momentum sends me headfirst into the boards.

There's no time to register what just happened before the world goes black.

29

HARLOW

It was bad enough, watching Ash hit the boards that way. Gasps ring out all around me, and I doubt I will ever forget the sick sensation that washed over me all at once when he made impact.

But it's the way he doesn't move that gets me on my feet with my heart lodged in my throat. No. No, not like this. This is not the way it's supposed to be.

All gameplay comes to a halt as the medical crew steps onto the ice, where several team members – including Ryder and Soren – have gathered around their fallen teammate.

Get up. Get up. It's only when there's a sharp pain in my palms that I realize I'm clenching my fists tight enough that my nails are almost breaking skin. He has to get up. He just has to.

But he's not. I can hardly breathe as I watch the medics load him onto a stretcher. I'm out of the row and on my way to the parking lot without giving it a second thought, and by the time I'm behind the wheel, the ambulance is starting out for the hospital. I follow behind, blinking back tears and praying to whoever or whatever cares to listen. Please, let him be safe. Please, let him be okay.

A thousand ugly fears race through my head in the time it takes to reach the hospital, where I park in front of the ER before sprinting inside. It takes a while before I'm able to get anybody's attention, but once I do, the nurse behind the desk asks an important question I was too busy freaking out to anticipate. "What's your relation to the patient?"

Dammit. They aren't going to come out and tell me what I want to hear without having a good reason. "I'm part of the medical staff for the team." I mean, it's not a lie, not really. I am part of the team's staff, and I am a doctor.

"It looks like they took him straight into imaging for an x-ray. You can wait in his berth until they bring him back, if you want." She directs me to an empty, curtained-off portion of the ER, where there's nothing for me to do but pace and bite my nails and wish I had said all the things I didn't get to say before now. There're so many regrets, I hardly know which one to focus on first.

And there's plenty of time to go through all of my many mistakes, since it feels like forever before the curtain parts and a man in scrubs comes my way. "I understand you're part of the team's medical staff? One of the nurses told me you were waiting in here."

"How is he?"

He doesn't need to say it in words. It's the way he grimaces before scrubbing a hand over his face that tells me my worst fears might come true. Now, I don't want him to say a word. I don't want to hear it.

"It could've been much worse, but it's still not great," he tells me.

"Is he…" I can't bring myself to say it. I can't even entertain the thought. Not Ash. Not when he's so healthy and vital, and when he loves hockey so much. It would be too cruel for him to lose what matters most in his life.

"Best we can tell right now, he has a severe concussion."

The memory of the way he slammed head first into the boards sets my teeth on edge and makes me shudder from head to toe. Of course, he has a severe concussion after something like that.

I sense there's more, and the doctor's soft sigh confirms it. "And according to the tests we've run, it looks like he has a torn ligament in his neck."

That's not nearly as bad as this could've been, but it's not exactly great news, either. Right away, all sorts of scenarios start to play out in my head. "He'll need therapy, I guess?"

"Oh, yes. He will. Quite a lot of it. And that's on top of whatever damage the concussion might have done. He's got a long road ahead of him."

I am here as a representative of the team. A medical professional. Not as his ex-girlfriend. I have to remember that, or else I'll end up blubbering all over the place. "Can I see him?"

"We're still running more tests to be on the safe side – and he is not clear headed enough that he would be able to have a conversation or anything like that. But he's in good hands."

"I understand." I hate the idea, but I understand.

"Is his family aware of this?"

Good question. "I'll have to call over to the arena and see about that." If anything, it's something to take my mind off of the gnawing fear that's taken root in my gut. What if he's never the same?

Before we part ways, I have to ask the last, biggest question left now that I have an idea of his condition. "Between you and me, will he play hockey again?"

It's not what he says. It's how long it takes him to say it. The way he hesitates, and the regret that hangs in his voice when he finally does speak. "That, I can't say for sure. A lot of it rides on how well he takes to therapy and the progress he makes there. It's going to take a lot of time, but he's young and strong."

That's still not an answer. "In your professional opinion, though?"

"In my opinion?" His brows draw together and his mouth tips down at the corners. "I wouldn't let a kid of mine play hockey. It's too dangerous. I've seen too many serious injuries, including concussions like his. Pro football isn't the only sport where players are prone to Chronic traumatic encephalopathy."

I know what he's talking about; CTE, the progressive and fatal brain disease associated with repeated traumatic brain injuries, including concussions and repeated blows to the head.

Nausea churns in my stomach and I have to bite my lip. It's hard to keep from getting emotional.

"Between you and me," he concludes as he backs away, "I'm not optimistic. But who knows?" And that's how he leaves me, standing alone, with my heart shattered in pieces all around me. I can't stand the idea of him not being able to play the sport he loves, something that's such a huge part of him. But what if my feelings don't matter? Because they don't, in the end. It doesn't matter that I want him to be healthy and well. It's not in my hands.

There's nothing I can do but wait for the inevitable arrival of the coach and whichever players decide to head over here and see how he's doing.

Something tells me I know who two of them will be – and right now, I need them more than I ever have.

30

HARLOW

Ash looks just like his dad. That's the first thing that runs through my head when his family makes it to the hospital. His mom is softer, with pale blue eyes that are now bloodshot after what I imagine was a very emotional ride out here. Her husband walks beside her, an arm around her waist like he's holding her up – but his clenched jaw and the narrowed gaze he wears tells me he might need a little support, too.

I don't have a chance to introduce myself before another set of elevator doors opens, allowing Coach Kozak to burst into the hallway, looking like he's close to exploding as he rushes down the hall. But he notices Ash's family and slows down, talking quietly with them before noticing me sitting in a chair outside Ash's room.

I haven't gone in. I'm not sure why, but somehow it doesn't feel like it's my place to be there right now. His family should see him first, if not the coach. I don't think his parents even notice me as they pass by, too busy worrying about their son. I wish there were something I could say to ease what they must be going through, but I get the feeling any words would come out flat and useless. I mean, what would I say, anyway? I'm sorry your son might never play hockey again? Hey, at least he didn't end up paralyzed? Even thinking those words makes me cringe.

"Doc." The coach places a hand on my shoulder. "How are you holding up?"

"Me? I'm fine. I'm not the one in the hospital bed right now."

"I spoke to the doctor downstairs, the one who treated him when he first came in."

That would explain the sorrow etched in every line of his face. "So you know what he thinks."

"At the end of the day, it doesn't matter what he thinks. It matters what Ash thinks he's capable of. Mind over matter, right?"

Because it seems like he needs me to, I give him as sincere a smile as I can muster. "You're right. There are times when all the physical therapy in the world can't help as much as a positive mindset."

"Of course! Who knows what might happen? He's a strong, determined kid. He'll be just fine." It's sweet of him to be so positive, but part of me wonders if he's not trying to convince himself along with me. He needs to. Otherwise, he just watched the end of a talented player's career.

"Are you alright?" I ask him.

"Me? I'm fine." When I lift an eyebrow, he lowers his gaze to the floor. "That's not an easy thing to watch. And the first thing I thought was, I was just screaming at him about getting penalized. I wondered if that was the last time I ever spoke to him. I regretted it."

"He started a fight out there," I remind him gently. "It was sort of your job to holler at him."

"Just the same. That's never how you want to end things with a person."

Do not cry. Not here. Not now. For the second time today, I dig my nails into my palm hard enough to hurt, but it helps take my mind off the emotion clogging my throat. We didn't end things so well, either, did we? He's probably still furious with me – at least, he was back when it mattered. An accident like his has a way of rearranging a person's priorities.

Over the next ten or fifteen minutes, the hallway starts to fill with other team members. My heart hurts when I see Ryder and Soren among them, and it takes pretty much all of my control not to throw myself into their arms and cry my heart out. Not the time, not the place. Besides, I doubt they would appreciate it much. We haven't exactly settled anything, after all.

The only thing I can do is sit here, feeling lost and scared and full of regret. That's what hurts the most. All the regret. All the *what if's* rolling through my head one after another like train cars.

It's Soren who finally approaches me, scuffing his toe against the tile floor and looking nervous. "Hi," he murmurs quietly enough that only I hear him over the mixed conversation going on all around us.

"Hi."

"How are you?"

Funny how it's a matter of reflex, opening my mouth to tell him I'm fine. Why wouldn't I be? Ash will be fine after some therapy. Life will go on.

But when I open my mouth to rattle this off, the only thing that comes out is a choked sob that bursts out of me all at once, probably because I've been holding it back all this time.

"Come with me." There's no room for argument once he takes me by the hand and pulls me to my feet. "You could probably use some air." He leads me to the elevator, and once we reach the ground floor, he directs me outside toward a little garden where a small fountain gurgles peacefully. Something about the tranquility of it all helps me release a little of the tension that has me in its grip. I sit down with a sigh, folding my hands in my lap and staring down at them.

"How are you, really?" he asks, sitting on the other side of the bench.

"I'm sad," I admit. "I'm worried. I am…" *Sorry. I am so, so sorry.* This isn't the time for that, and I don't deserve his comfort right now. Not when his best friend is lying in a bed. He is the one who needs understanding and compassion, not me.

"I'm worried, too. That was some scary shit out there today."

"I felt so helpless."

"I know. Like watching a nightmare come to life, and there's nothing you can do to stop it."

"Exactly. And then they put him on the stretcher…"
I shiver at the memory, and he reaches out to pat my
shoulder. It's a little awkward, but it feels nice. Even
a simple touch like that.

"There have been guys who've come back from
much worse than this, sometimes even better than
they were before. Let's not count him out just yet."

"Oh, I know. I do. I just wish it didn't have to be like
this."

"It's a shame wishing won't get us anywhere."
There's no bitterness in his voice. More like a sad
resignation. I don't think I've ever heard him speak
so seriously before. It's almost like I'm sitting with
the real Soren right now, with all the jokes and the
sarcasm stripped away. What a shame it took
something like this for him to drop the act.

"How have you been?" he murmurs. His arm is
extended along the back of the bench, and every
once in a while his fingers brush my hair or the back
of my neck. I don't have it in me to ask him to stop,
mostly because I don't want him to stop. It's like
every touch brings me closer to myself.

"I've been…" *Lonely. Miserable. Worried about all of you.
Trying like hell to justify my decision.* "Busy."

"Sure. You're trying to wrangle all of us and keep us
playing well together. I wouldn't want your job."

"And how about you?" Even feeling as low as I am, I can't help teasing him a little. "I heard you've been back out there, dating around."

I'm surprised when he grimaces a little before turning his attention to the fountain gurgling in front of us. "I'm trying to move on. I can't spend the rest of my life missing you the way I do now."

It's not like I didn't know he would miss me, but hearing him say it out loud is sort of nice. I've heard too many rumors lately about him getting around, being seen with a different girl just about every night. Does it make me jealous? Sure. And I've had to wonder how he could so easily go from being with me to being with some other random girl.

It's like he's reading my thoughts when he turns my way, looking sheepish. "They don't mean anything. I want you to know that."

"You don't have to —"

"Please. Let me get this off my chest." I force myself to keep my mouth shut, even if a whole bunch of word vomit wants to come pouring out. "None of those girls mean anything. Just a lot of one-night stands I hardly remember now. I've been trying like hell to get you out of my system, but all it does is make me miss you more. It's not easy for me to admit that," he adds, "But I want you to know. I can't just forget about you. There is no forgetting about you."

I should tell him to try harder. I should tell him there's no point in feeling anything for me. But that would be cruel – not to mention a big, fat lie. Because, of course, I still want him. I still want to be with him, with all of them. I wouldn't be doing either of us any favors if I pretended otherwise.

"I miss you, too," I whisper. "All of you. You have no idea how much. And what I did… I didn't want to. I hope you understand that. I did what I thought was best for everybody."

"I understand. I do, really. You did what you thought was right. We don't have to always like doing what's right."

"Sometimes, we can hate it," I agree, and he chuckles like he understands.

Right now, it's enough. Sitting together like this, connecting again, when we're both hurting and worried… I think it's what we both need.

31

RYDER

"You're not serious. That can't be true."

Max shrugs and looks as miserable as I feel. "That's what I heard. That's what the doctor said."

"But he couldn't have meant Ash will never play again. That's impossible."

"I'm only telling you what the doctor thinks, man." He grinds his teeth and grunts like he's angry. "I don't like it, either. It fucking sucks, and I hope he's wrong."

He needs to be wrong. That's all there is to it. There's no way Ash won't play again. Not him. Not like this.

His room is too full right now for me to go in and say hi, but I can see him from where I'm standing near the door. He's got one of those collars around his neck to keep his head still, and he's got all sorts of tubes and sensors and whatnot attached at various places. He must hate it — though if he's got the kind of concussion the doctor is talking about, he might not even know what's going on. The idea hurts. It hurts a lot.

Just like it will hurt him if he finds out his career ended today.

I don't want to think about it. I want to push the idea out of my head with both hands and lock the door behind it. No way. There's just no way. Not Ash. He's too good to go out like this. He loves it too much.

It's childish, thinking things like that. Of course it's possible. This kind of thing happens all the time. And somewhere in the back of our minds, we all know it. We have to. No, we can't, like, dwell on it all the time or else we would never play up to our full potential. We'd be too worried about getting hurt. Nobody ever won a game while they were all caught up in whether or not they'd get hurt. The possibility is always out there, hanging over our heads.

It's just that I've never known anybody personally who's gone down like this. It was never one of my friends. One of my teammates.

And all of a sudden I feel a lot more vulnerable than I did before. What would I do if it were me in that bed? Hockey saved my life. It gave me something to reach for. A goal. How would I have turned out without it? I shudder to think. It wouldn't have been pretty.

Life is too short to get caught up in bullshit. I already knew that deep down inside, but it's times like this when it's more obvious than ever. Tomorrow is never guaranteed. Ash could've died out there today. All it would've taken was hitting the boards at a slightly different angle, and he could've snapped his neck. And I would never have been able to tell him how sorry I am that things sort of fell apart for all of us. I would never have been able to apologize for taking my jealousy out on him. I would've had to carry the memory of our ruined friendship with me for the rest of my life.

It's like having a second chance now, in a way. I'm not going to waste it. From now on, there's no petty bullshit. We're not letting personal stuff get between us anymore.

I'm too anxious to hang around outside his room, so I start to wander a little. I need to get rid of this nervous energy. Besides, being around so many people who don't really understand what went down between us isn't helping anything. I can't really relate to how they're feeling when it's much more complex for me.

At the end of the hall, there's a bank of vending machines – and standing in front of them is one person who gets it.

Fuck, I want to hold her. I might even want her to hold me. I'm so screwed up inside. I can't stop remembering how it felt to stand there as one awful second after another ticked by without Ash moving. Wondering if he was dead. Knowing it could easily have been me.

She notices my reflection in the glass and turns around. "Hi."

It feels kind of hollow when there's so much more I want to say, but it's as good a place to start as any. "Hey. How are you holding up?"

"I'm fine. I'm not the one in a hospital bed."

"Yeah. It's... pretty fucked up."

"You're a real poet." But she's smiling a little, and that's a good thing. "How are you?"

"I'm fine, Doc. No need to shrink me."

"I wasn't trying to." She looks and sounds wounded, and I wish I hadn't said it.

"That was an awkward joke. Sorry. I don't know how to be."

"I understand." All at once, her eyes light up. "So what's this with your foster brother? I wanted to ask about him. How did that happen?"

I guess it's a safe subject, and I'll talk about anything so long as it means being able to stand here with her. "He's a good kid, but he's messed up. Not in any, you know, permanent kind of way. He's got a chip on his shoulder."

Her lips twitch in the beginnings of a smile. "Now who does that remind me of?"

"I guess that's why I've always been able to get through to him, because I understand him. Only right now…"

I lean against one of the machines with a sigh. It feels good, getting this off my chest, even if it feels strange to be talking about it when it's Ash we're here for. "I just don't know if I have it in me to be, like, a father figure or whatever he needs. I don't have the first clue. It's one thing when you're sharing a house and you have foster parents with you, and it's another thing to talk on the phone when you're on the other side of the country. But now, he's at my house, and I have to set the rules, and I don't have the first idea what the hell I'm doing."

"I don't know. From what I saw at the store, you were doing a good job. Making sure he has what he needs."

"That's nothing."

"That's not true. Everybody needs to feel like somebody cares enough to go out of their way to provide for them. Just one person, that's all it takes. And you're his person."

I see what she means. But... "I don't know if I'll be a good influence. I don't know if I'll end up helping him, or screwing him up."

"I've never had kids of my own, obviously, but I can tell you no parent knows if they're going to do a good job. They can only do their best." She laughs softly and shakes her head. "I've been telling myself to be more understanding of my parents for pretty much my entire life, don't forget. The best I can do is tell myself they're trying."

"I guess I see what you mean."

"He's lucky to have somebody in his life who cares as much as you do."

"We'll see if he feels lucky once I start setting down ground rules."

"Nobody wants to be the bad guy."

"Exactly."

"You'll be just fine." She reaches out and touches my arm and for one crazy second I want to tell her everything. How much I miss her. How I want her back. How there are nights when all I can do is lie in bed and crave her. Not just sexually, but in general. Even something as simple and innocent as this conversation reminds me of everything I'm missing without her in my life. Her quiet, constant support. The warmth of her smile. Her solid advice. I miss... her.

But telling her that now would be pointless, not to mention pathetic. I don't want to make it look like I'm taking advantage of a shit situation.

"Thank you," I murmur instead, which means leaving everything I'm thinking and feeling unspoken. The last thing she needs is to handle my bullshit.

32

ASH

"Let me help you into the car."

"I can do it on my own." The words are barely out of my mouth before I regret them. I don't need to see the wounded look on my mom's face to feel like a piece of shit for snapping at her, but it doesn't help.

"Sorry," I mumble as I ease myself to the passenger seat. I can't even drive. I can't do a damn thing on my own.

"You're just frustrated." I manage to wait until she's closed the door to walk around to the driver's side before I growl. It's one thing to feel completely helpless. It's another to be babied and patronized, which is exactly how I feel every time she or Dad or Amy says something like that. Like I'm a child again.

Like they have to watch what they say around me and make excuses for me. I don't want that. I don't want any of this.

But she's right. I am damn frustrated. Two weeks after I left the hospital, and I still need too much help to be left on my own. It's like I had to step back in time. Like I'm a kid again, relying on my parents for everything.

So yeah, I kind of want to tear somebody's head off on a daily basis.

"Amy called me earlier." When all I do is grunt, Mom continues. "She asked how you were doing."

"Did you tell her I'm not much different than I was yesterday when she asked?"

"What do you expect? She's your sister. She's concerned for you, just like we all are."

Stop being concerned. It would hurt her if I said it, so I keep it to myself. I don't always — sometimes I'm too damn frustrated and pissed off to think before I speak. I'm not proud of the way I've acted.

But dammit, it's days like this when I wonder whether I'll ever be healthy again. That's terrifying. Not even because it would mean never playing the game again — though that would be bad enough. I worry I'll never be able to live alone again. I'll never be independent. There are still days when I wake up and my memory is foggy. I've already lost my shit more than once when my parents tried to be helpful and gave me the word I was struggling to remember. I don't want to be babied. I know they think they're being helpful, but they're driving me out of my skull.

And, of course, I feel like the world's biggest jackass for feeling this way. They didn't have to bring me home to take care of me here.

"Soren called."

I can't help but bristle, even though she announced it like it's a good thing. "He called the house?"

"Yes, he called the landline. What about it?"

"Did he forget my number?"

"No, Mr. Smart Mouth. He said you haven't been answering your phone. Why not?"

We're only a few minutes away from the therapy center, though we could still have another hour of driving ahead of us and it wouldn't be enough time to explain why I've been avoiding his calls. I can't imagine anybody would understand unless they were in this situation.

"Well?" Because of course, she's not going to let this go until I give her an answer.

"I don't know what to say. I don't feel like talking to anybody."

"I thought the two of you were so close."

"Yeah, when we have hockey in common."

"Who says you don't anymore?"

"Mom, come on. You're the one taking me to these therapy sessions. Can't you see how I'm struggling?"

"It's going to take time."

I want to scream every time I hear somebody say that. "It's already been two weeks."

"I have a newsflash for you, son. We heal on our body's time, and that's that. Going through therapy, doing your exercises at home, all of those things are helping speed the process."

Great. I hate to think of how much slower this would be if I weren't fumbling my way through therapy.

"Listen." She parks the car close to the entrance and turns to me, sighing. "I'm not going to pretend I understand exactly how you feel. You're an athlete. You've always been able to rely on your body. I can only imagine that must make this worse."

Hell yes, it does. Things that used to come so easily to me take conscious effort now. I can't even bend down to tie my shoes yet. I can't get any exercise until the doctor clears me, and there's no telling how long that will take. I've always been able to rely on my body, and now there's nothing but darkness and confusion when I try imagining what the future holds. Right now, the best I can hope for is having a nurse with me to help with things even a child can do on their own.

And all because I was freaked out and panicking during the game.

"It's not easy," I agree, staring out the windshield. Somebody's coming out, using a walker to support themselves. I'm not that bad off, but I might as well be.

"One thing I've always admired about you is the way you never sit back feeling sorry for yourself even when things are tough."

I have to settle for side-eyeing her since I can't turn my head with this damn collar on my neck. I'm so sick of this thing, I can't describe it. "Am I in such bad shape that I need a pep talk like that?"

"You tell me when you're finished feeling sorry for yourself." She's out of the car before I can respond, and the way her lips twitch tell me she's feeling pretty proud of herself for that one. I won't ruin it by arguing.

Besides, I sort of need all my strength and focus to get through this session. I already know it's going to hurt, since it always does. Even simple actions like tipping my head to the side or bending forward while keeping my head level are practically impossible and painful as hell. Everybody keeps telling me I'm making progress, but I sure as hell don't feel like I am. I only feel pathetic and weak and useless.

And every day that passes without substantial improvement is like coming one day closer to the inevitable, finding out I'll never play again. I don't know what I would do if that's how it turns out. Mom wonders why I'm in such a hurry? That's why. I need to get better, because I need to play. It's all I've ever wanted to do, the only plan I ever had for my life. Everything else, I figured I would take care of as it came up. But hockey was always at the center of everything.

What now? Where do I go? What do I do when I'm not prepared for anything else after being single-minded for so many years?

I've seen players from all different sports after they've had to retire much earlier than they ever figured they would. I've seen what that can do. How it can wear a person down until they aren't even a shadow of who they used to be. They're haunted.

Haunted by the past and by a future that will never come true. Is that what I have to look forward to now? And what if it is? What do I do then?

"Right on time." My therapist is a good guy. He means well. But right now, I don't feel like returning his smile as we enter the center. "Ready to do some work today?"

"Doesn't matter if I'm ready or not." He gives me a good-natured laugh, then directs me to a chair while Mom hangs back, leaning against the wall. Now, she can look as worried as she feels without me seeing it. She won't have to pretend to be positive and hopeful for my sake. And I don't have to pretend I'm feeling positive just so she'll feel better.

"You know the drill. Let's start stretching you out."

He makes it sound so easy, but then this used to be easy for me. Now, I have an hour of pain and frustration to look forward to. An hour of feeling useless.

But who am I kidding? That's how I feel every minute of the day.

And there's no end in sight.

So, I grit my teeth and go through it anyway, because I'll be damned if I give up.

33

HARLOW

I don't know what I expected when I received the invitation to the party at Ash's house today. From what I understand, he only moved back in a few days ago – I guess he couldn't stand living with his parents anymore, but then I can't imagine moving back in with mine, either. Even for the reason he did. He's spent years being independent, calling the shots for himself.

In other words, he must've been in a pretty big hurry. I've spent the past few days hoping he's not taking it too fast. It's barely been six weeks since his injury. He could end up hurting himself even worse if he pushes himself too hard.

There are plenty of cars parked at the curb, and the sounds of laughter coming from the backyard when I ring the doorbell. I haven't seen him since that day, lying in the bed after a doctor told me they weren't sure whether he would ever be able to play again. I guess that's why I'm so nervous and twitchy as I wait for somebody to open the door.

"Hey!" Before I know what's happening, Ash is hugging me — gently, professionally, if there is a professional way to hug somebody. "I'm glad you came! I was hoping you would."

He holds me at arm's length and laughs softly. "What's the matter? You look like you've seen a ghost."

I sort of feel like I have. The ghost of the Ash I used to know and thought I would never see again. He looks terrific, strong and energetic.

"Come on in. I don't know if you got the chance to meet my parents at the hospital, but I'm sure they would like to meet you." I must look terrified, because he laughs gently before leaning in to murmur in my ear. "Don't worry. They don't know anything. You're just the team therapist."

Well, that's good to know. I wouldn't want to find out he started blabbing with a bunch of painkillers in his system.

Most of the team is already here, including the players my eyes immediately search for. I can't help it. It's reflex at this point. They're out by the pool, chatting near the grill, while a man I recognize as Ash's dad flips chicken and burgers. Ash's mom wanders around making sure people have what they need, while a girl who can only be Amy loads the dishwasher. She takes after their mom the way Ash is almost a mirror of his dad.

"I told them I don't need any help, but they ignored me." There's fondness in Ash's voice, though, and I could cry at the sound of it. I've been getting conflicting reports the past several weeks – Soren told me during one of our sessions that he couldn't get Ash on the phone, and worrying about him was starting to affect Soren's gameplay. The same thing was true of several other players who were shaken up after what they saw and what they heard at the hospital.

But it seems like all of that is in the past. I fix myself a plate and greet the people I recognize before heading out to the back patio. I can't help it. It's like there's a magnet pulling me toward them.

"Feeling any better?" I murmur to Soren.

"It's like a miracle," he marvels, watching Ash over the top of my head. "He's like his old self."

"I was thinking the same thing."

"I was talking with him earlier, and he said he's back to working out and everything. He's even been running." Ryder looks and sounds impressed, and I know how he feels.

Still… "I hope he's not pushing it too hard."

"The doctor cleared him," Soren points out with a shrug as the three of us sit down at one of the folding tables set up for the party.

It's only a few minutes before Ash joins us. His smile is wide and warm as he settles in with a plate of chicken and salad. "Amy kicked me out of the kitchen and told me to go sit down," he explains with a grin. "I figured it was a good idea to listen."

"You don't want to overdo it," I remind him as gently as I possibly can. I don't want to insult him, but I feel like it needs to be said.

"I know, I know. Believe me, I'm not trying to fuck myself over for good by pushing it too hard. But I feel great. I really do. I'm working out again and everything."

"And you're well enough to come back home, so you must feel great." My heart swells until it practically lodges in my throat, though that could be the emotion that keeps threatening to work its way out of me in the form of happy tears. He's better than I dared let myself imagine.

And as we sit together, chatting over beers and food, it's like we fall back into our old routine in a way. All the awkwardness and bitterness has dissolved, and left behind is the chemistry that brought us together in the first place. My ribs ache by the time I'm finished laughing at the banter going on between the three of them, but I welcome the feeling, because it means having them back — even if we can only be friends. I'll take it.

Amy needs to get back to school, and her parents are going to drive her back, meaning they need to head out before everything is cleaned up. "Don't worry about that. I can help out," I offer when Ash's mom looks worried.

"Would you? That would be such a big help. I hate the idea of leaving him alone with all that work."

"You know I can hear you," he calls out from the kitchen. "And last I checked, I remember how to work a dishwasher." She rolls her eyes, but there's a happy smile tugging at her mouth by the time she leaves. The house is pretty much emptied out now, and the sun is starting to set as I gather what's left on the patio, tossing paper napkins and plastic cups into a trash bag. Really, most of what they used is disposable – less work, I guess – so it doesn't take long before I have my end of things squared away.

I bring the trash bag inside, and Ryder adds a few things from the living room. There are serving trays sitting on the island and I pick them up and place them on the counter for Ash to rinse them off before they go in the dishwasher.

"It's nice seeing you like this. All domestic, and whatnot." He growls softly at my comment and I giggle before turning away to look for anything else that needs cleaning up.

All I get for it is a sudden cold sensation in the center of my back.

"Are you serious?" I shriek while I jump a mile and spin around to find Ash holding the sprayer from the sink. "What did I ever do to you?"

"That's what you get for being a smart ass." He sprays me again, and this time the water hits my chest.

"You dick!" I scramble around to the other side of the island to put myself out of range.

"What? Are you afraid of a little water?"

"I'm not trying to turn this into a wet t-shirt contest, you jerk."

"Okay. Fine." I'm glad when he returns the sprayer to its mount... but that doesn't stop him from stalking slowly around the island, his eyes gleaming with a light I recognize all too well.

When I tense, ready to run, he clicks his tongue. "Come on, now. Would you make a man in my condition run around after you?" I'm about to call him a few pretty unpleasant names when he reaches out and grabs me by the waist, hauling me in close. I would say I didn't expect it, but I'm not going to lie to myself. I can feel the change in the air. I can sense what's on his mind. And while on one hand, it's nice to know he's feeling well enough to even consider us getting close to each other, that still doesn't make it right.

Even if it feels very, very right when he kisses me.

Wrong, this is all wrong, you need to stop this. Sure. I know I do. All the old reasons come flooding back – ethics, and our futures and all of that.

Right now, though? It doesn't really matter, because I almost lost him. It's situations like this that can remind a person how fragile life is, how we can't take anything for granted.

And that's why I sink into his kiss with no regret, no misgivings. I melt against him with a happy sigh, parting my lips so his tongue can slip between them and light me on fire. My heart might explode, and my panties might melt off, but I won't be sorry. I'm so tired of being sorry for wanting what I want.

"Well, shit. This is what I miss when I'm trying to be helpful."

Funny how my heart was racing only a second ago, and now it wants to stop when I hear Soren's voice. I pull away in time to find both him and Ryder watching with their arms folded.

"Sorry." Ash shrugs, smirking. "I couldn't resist."

They wouldn't fight again, would they? Not after everything that's happened.

Ryder and Soren exchange a meaningful look before Soren crosses the room, his fists swinging at his sides. *No, no, not like this. Not again.*

Then he smiles. I barely have time to be relieved before he buries his hands in my hair and kisses me more deeply than Ash did. He takes his time, moving slowly, leaving me wet and aching and whimpering for more by the time he lets me up for air.

"My turn." I gasp in surprise when Ryder wedges himself between me and Soren so he can kiss me hard, deep, until my lips sting and ache from the force. But it's not enough to make me stop him. It's just the opposite. Something hot and needy inside me flares to life, and I reach out and take his shirt in my fists to pull him closer once the surprise melts away and is replaced by need. I've been so alone, so lonely. I need them so much.

Enough that I'm almost able to forget how wrong it is. *Almost.*

34

ASH

Am I dreaming? I must be, since I was sure this would never happen again. I told myself to get used to knowing I would never touch her, never kiss her, never know the sensation of my pulse pounding in anticipation of what's about to happen next. I tried to get her out of my system, I did, I know we all did. Yet here we are, having worked our way upstairs to my room in the middle of so many kisses and caresses. Somehow we made it here, and now Harlow is tumbling onto my bed, already pulling off her sleeveless sweater before leaning back to unbutton her jeans.

This is everything I wanted. Everything I thought I would never have again. It's not just that she's here, eager and ready to go. It's me.

I was afraid I wouldn't get back to this place where my body's ready. I didn't get an erection the entire first two weeks after the injury – I was too fucked up, in pain and taking meds whenever it got to be too much. Nothing was working the way it should, and there were a few moments when I feared they never would again.

But here I am, with a raging hard on and the urge to sink it deep inside her as soon as possible. I've never needed anything more.

Even so, when I've pulled my t-shirt over my head and begin crawling across the bed to where she waits, she sits up all at once and frowns. At the sight of that, all activity stops — Soren was in the middle of taking off his pants, and so was Ryder, but they freeze.

"What's wrong?" Soren asks.

"Are you sure you're well enough to do this?" Her hand is trembling when she reaches out to stroke my cheek. "I don't want you to overdo it."

Like I didn't already know I love her. Emotion tightens my throat and for one wild second, I want to tell her out loud in front of the guys that I still love her. I never stopped. I've never loved her more than I do now.

But I can't find the words. Instead of answering, I kiss her palm, then lower her hand until she's cupping my aching bulge. "Does this answer your question?" I rasp, gritting my teeth against the sheer heat of her touch.

She bites her lip and lust flares to life in her eyes, but it's not enough to wipe away her doubt. "I don't want you to hurt yourself."

Soren slides in next to her, grinning at me before murmuring in her ear. "We'll take it slow. Nice and easy." When his tongue makes contact with her earlobe, she shudders and whimpers and lies back, holding her arms out to me and lifting her hips so I can work her jeans down her legs.

At first, it's enough to explore her again. I soak in the softness of her skin, running my hands over her legs and ass. Ryder unclasps her bra and right away descends on one of her full tits, groaning when he takes her nipple into his mouth. She runs her fingers through his hair, moaning louder when Soren does the same on the other side.

I drape one of her legs over my shoulder and run my tongue over her skin, worshiping her, determined to give her all the pleasure she can take after holding back for so long. For a while, it's enough to play, to taste and touch while she loses herself a little bit at a time. Ours. She'll always be ours.

And we'll always be hers. When she opens her eyes and her gaze locks on mine, I know it. No matter how any of us tries to stop this, it's no use. There is no breaking this up.

The heat radiating from her gets my dick dripping, or maybe that's nothing more than the thrill of doing this again after such a long, dry spell. She wraps her slim fingers around my shaft and fuck me, I could weep. "Take it easy," I whisper through gritted teeth. "It's been a while, and I don't want to blow it this early."

"I'll take it easy on you," she purrs, and there's nothing I can do but close my eyes and give myself over to the pure bliss she's sending through my body with every stroke. "Shit, that's nice," I groan, letting my head fall back while the sounds of pleasure fill the room. *Finally*.

"Why don't you lie down?" she asks me, and the guys back away so she can get up to let me take her place. "Just lie back."

Who am I to argue with something like that? I am too glad to lie on my back so she can straddle my hips. The heat from her pussy leaves me gritting my teeth again, fighting off the urge to let go. Not yet. It's been a while, but not yet. I want to savor this.

I watch, holding my breath, while she positions herself over me. The sight of my wide head disappearing inside her is spellbinding, and the feeling of her tight muscles clenching around me is enough to make fireworks burst in my head. "Holy shit," I whisper, and the urge to lose myself and give in to release is stronger than ever. I forgot how good this is. How could I forget?

"You feel so good…" she moans, letting her head fall back, her mouth hanging open so she can suck in quick breaths before she starts to move — slowly, sensually, like she is savoring every inch as I move inside her.

"Fuck, that's hot." Ryder kneels behind her, taking her tits in his hands and sucking her neck. She leans against him, moaning her approval as she rocks her hips and grinds against me.

"That's right." Soren stands beside the bed, stroking himself and watching intently. "You fuck him. Fuck him nice and slow. Get yourself good and wet. Make yourself come." I know his words are meant for her, but they spread fresh fire through me, too.

I look down between us and watch my shaft disappear again and again, coated with her juices. It's not enough. I want her all over me. I have never been so completely lost over a woman. I didn't know it was possible to crave this connection as deeply as I do. I didn't know such intense, mind-blowing pleasure was possible, either.

It's more than simple pleasure. It's connection. Something so deep, it almost scares me a little. Needing her like I need air. Needing this, all of us together. I don't know what to call it. I only know I am never as comfortable or as sure of myself as I am when we're like this, locked together, touching and feeling and following our bodies' needs.

My soul's needs, too.

"So good... Oh, my God..." Her hips start to jerk frantically around the time her muscles tighten around me. Fuck, yes, she's so close. So am I. I don't know how much longer I can last. It's been weeks, after all, and jerking off is no replacement for having her wrapped around me like this. It's just not the same.

Ryder lets go of her and she falls on top of me, blocking out the rest of the world when her hair falls to either side of my face. It's us, it's only us, and she stares into my eyes for a beat before our mouths meet and her thrusts become more frantic. Sheer animal lust explodes in me and I give myself over to it, jerking my hips to meet her thrusts. My fingers dig into her hips to pull her down harder, faster, until she goes still and screams into my mouth a heartbeat before her muscles flutter, massaging me, milking me.

Rather than come inside her before everyone's had their turn I lift her hips. She releases me with a gasp — then takes me in her mouth all at once, her head bobbing rapidly, her tongue massaging me the way her pussy did.

And I'm gone. Release rushes over me all at once, and I give into it finally, almost sobbing in relief while emptying my balls down her throat. My ears are ringing and my heart's racing out of control by the time she lifts her head. I feel like I just went through a hurricane.

And I don't think I've ever been happier.

35

SOREN

I don't know what it is about watching Ash letting go like that. This is more than getting off on watching somebody else fuck. I'm happy for him, glad he has come back from his injury, and I can practically feel his relief once he lets go. It's always a relief to finally come after fighting it off, but this is bigger than that. This is the first time with her after the accident. After we feared we could never be with her again. That adds a whole new layer over and above what must already feel so good. Mind blowing, even.

It's strange, the emotion that wells up in me. Something much deeper than lust, for sure. She's ours, she's really ours. We're together again. I will never take this for granted, even if today is all we ever have. It will have to be enough.

And when I think about it that way, my hunger grows. As soon as Harlow has released Ash's dick, I'm on her, thrusting a hand between her legs and finding her hot and wet. She purrs and melts against me, winding her arms around my neck while bearing down on my fingers.

Ash lies back and watches while he catches his breath. Ryder, meanwhile, kneels behind her again. For a while, it's enough for us to take turns kissing her, touching and pleasing her, pulling one moan after another from deep in her core. I glance over at Ash and find him watching and wearing a crooked grin. When his gaze falls on me, the grin widens, and I smile back. At the end of the day, no matter what happens, we have this to come back to. This connection.

How much longer will we have it?

Maybe it's the uncertainty that's getting to me. Maybe that's what makes this all feel so much more profound than it normally would. I tried to convince myself I could get along without ever doing this again, but I was kidding myself. And I would be kidding myself again if I pretended I could move on after tonight. No, all she's doing is reminding me of how necessary she is. Not just for me, either. For all of us.

We're a tangle of arms and legs by the time Harlow closes her hand around me and begins to stroke what was already rigid and throbbing. "Let me put this in my mouth," she whispers. Nothing in the world could convince me to say no. I back up, giving her room to get on her knees on the bed while I stand in front of her. Has there ever been anything as sexy as this woman when she's on her hands and knees and smiling wickedly at me?

Yes, there is, and that's when her tongue darts out and she drags it around the ridge of my head. How is it possible that she makes it feel so good? How does she light me up inside while waking my endless hunger? I'm torn between affection and pure, savage lust as I sink my hands into her hair and groan her name. "You're so good to me," I mutter, moving my hips to offer more of myself to her waiting mouth.

I expect Ryder to take her from behind – he's right there, in position, and it's what I would do. Instead, he surprises everyone by lying on his back and inching his way between her thighs until she is poised over his face. She lets out a surprised noise that's barely stifled by my dick, but Ryder only responds by wrapping his arms around her thighs and pulling her down so she has no choice but to settle on top of him.

"Shit, why didn't I think of that?" Ash is starting to get hard again, stroking himself with his eyes glued to what's happening on the bed. Harlow's deep, guttural moans are followed by the grinding of her hips — and the suction from her mouth increases almost like it's a response to what Ryder is doing with his tongue. He sounds like he's in heaven, grunting and groaning, panting like an animal in heat. Lucky bastard.

My dick is moving in and out of her mouth but I still kind of wish I were in his place. Next time, for sure.

If there is a next time. There has to be a next time.

"That's right. Ride his face," Ash mutters, stroking what's now fully erect while I slowly fuck Harlow's face. Lovingly, if it's possible to do this lovingly. I do love her. I didn't know how much until she broke things off.

She does as she's told, her hips rolling and grinding, and by the time her saliva starts dripping down my shaft I know she's too close to keep from getting sloppy. That's why I pull out, stroking myself in front of her face while she cries out her impending orgasm.

"Come on his face," I mutter, stroking her tits with one hand and myself with the other. She's almost too perfect, ripe and luscious and all ours — at least for tonight. "I want you to coat his face. Can you do that for me? Can you be a good girl?"

"Yes… Yes…!" And she throws her head back and howls while Ryder's satisfied grunts tell me she's doing exactly what I asked. Lucky bastard.

I can't take it. The sight and the sound of her ecstasy pushes me over the edge all at once. I'm barely able to direct myself to her open mouth before I coat her tongue with the first spurt. She takes it all, every bit of me, until I'm wiped out and my knees are shaking from the force.

And when I open my eyes and the world comes back into focus, she's smiling, lifting her hips so Ryder can slide out from under her. Any thoughts of taking a break are swept away when he takes her by the hips and drives himself into her from behind.

She lets out a startled gasp but pushes back against him. "I need you to fuck me," she begs, her voice shaking the way her body does. She's barely come down from her orgasm, and already she wants more.

And Ryder is happy to oblige, pounding her hard enough to rock the bed while she screams her approval. "Just like that! Yes, yes, harder!" There's sweat beading on his brow but he obeys, the way any man with half a brain would do when a woman like her shouts an order like that.

"Yes! Yes, Ryder!" Her howls fill the room before she almost collapses, while he pulls out and comes across her ass. I crouch beside her, stroking her hair, kissing her cheek and forehead until he's finished and she's still whimpering from the force of her release.

Her eyes open slowly. There's a hazy look about them, almost like she's drowsy. "I can't believe I missed out on that," she admits in a rasping whisper.

"You know, I was thinking the same thing." I look away from her long enough to find Ash stroking himself faster while Ryder heads to the bathroom. I assume he intends to clean her up.

And I'm already starting to thicken again by the time Ash reaches out and runs a hand down her leg.

"Something tells me we're going to spend the rest of the night making up for lost time," I murmur, smiling at her. "I hope you don't mind."

When her drowsy grin widens, I know I have nothing to worry about.

36

RYDER

Damn birds. They're determined to wake me up this morning. I close my eyes tighter like that will do anything to block out sound and roll onto my side, determined not to let them win.

But that's before I remember where I am and what we did.

Right away, I reach for my phone, sitting on top of my folded jeans beside the couch where I slept last night. It sits beside the bed – king size, sure, yet still not quite enough room for four of us. But the couch is nice and long and very comfortable, and I've never been somebody who likes sharing a bed with another man. That's just not my thing. So it wasn't much of a sacrifice.

That's not what's on my mind as I check my phone. It's the first night I've left Pete alone at the house, but there weren't any panicked texts, so I'm guessing things went okay. I shoot him a quick message to let him know I'll be home later this morning, then let the phone drop from my fingers while I throw my arm over my head and wonder if it's worth trying to get back to sleep.

Last night was way beyond what I expected. I hoped, sure, but I didn't expect it. It was hot, it was exciting. It was also necessary, since the weeks I spent alone were pretty much torture.

I think it was necessary in other ways. It sort of brought us all back together.

Now, the only question is what happens next. Never an easy question, but especially in a situation like this. We still have to see each other all the time. And I don't know what I'll do if Harlow tries to convince us this can never happen again. It wouldn't be the first time.

But now more than ever, I know it will be impossible to act like we never happened. I can't live without this – I know that now. I mean, I'd go on, but it would all seem so empty and pointless without her. I can't believe I'm thinking this way as I lie here, trying to ignore the birds who have made it their life mission to keep me awake.

"Good morning."

My eyes snap open at Harlow's soft whisper. She's lying near the edge of the bed, close to me, wrapped in a blanket that barely covers her chest and with one of her legs peeking out. It doesn't seem possible for me to even consider screwing around again, but the sight of her smooth, soft leg gets me thinking in that direction anyway.

"Wait a second." I prop myself up on my elbow and look across the bed. Only Ash is lying next to her. "Where's Soren?"

"He went out for a run." She grins and lifts a shoulder when I scowl. "There I was, thinking he got enough of a workout last night. What do I know?"

Good for him. That's the last thing on my mind this morning. I've never been disciplined to the point of forcing myself to work out when I don't absolutely need to, like for work or whatever. All I want to do right now is be lazy and maybe think about last night.

There's no time for that, since Soren comes in moments later. "You're all still lying around?"

Ash grumbles before rolling onto his back with a sigh. "I wouldn't have had you stay over if I knew you were going to wake me up at the ass crack of dawn this morning."

"Seven o'clock is hardly the ass crack of dawn." He peels off his sweaty t-shirt and winks at Harlow. "Care to join me in the shower?"

"No way." Ash flings an arm around her and pulls her in close. "I'm not giving her up."

"I keep forgetting I have no say in anything." She clicks her tongue at him and shakes her head like she's disappointed, though I can see she's fighting a grin. "But no, thank you. Remember? It's everybody, or it's nobody."

All at once he gets serious, folding his arms and looking from Ash to me before turning his attention back to Harlow. "I was thinking on my run that we should maybe talk about this."

Ash throws an arm over his eyes. "Exactly what I feel like doing this morning. Talking."

"I'm just saying, maybe we should get the ground rules in place." Soren looks at Harlow like he is hoping for approval.

She sits up, frowning. "You know, he's right."

"Of course he is," Ash sighs.

"I'm serious."

"I know you are." He lowers his arm, then props himself up on his elbows and gives Soren a pretty filthy look. "Soren is always so thoughtful and helpful."

"Get over it," Soren tells him with a laugh. "Sorry to interrupt your beauty sleep."

Sitting up, I scrub my hands over my face, then over my hair while trying to get my brain moving. I expected this, just maybe not quite so soon. I usually need coffee before I can come anywhere close to thinking clearly.

Then again, there's not much to think about. "If we can, I want to get back together. We tried it your way, Harlow, and it just didn't work. I spent the entire time missing you too much to think about anything else. It was misery. I'm not ashamed to admit it." There. I said it and I didn't burst into flame or melt from shame.

"Same here," Ash grunts. "I hate to think of keeping things that way, though I understand why it was important to split up. But there's got to be another way we can do this."

Soren places himself on the foot of the bed, and he's not joking anymore. "Let's think about it. Now, we know there are bound to be setbacks. There's going to be tension — just like there is on the team. It's human nature. And we can't be naïve about it. There will be tension sometimes. There will be fights."

"Not about me, though. That's what I can't stand." She draws her knees to her chest and wraps her arms around her legs, peering at us through wide eyes. "Can you promise you won't fight about me? Gosh, that sounds so stupid."

"Why do you say that?" I ask.

"Because it's me. Like, why would you even fight over me? I can't even figure out why you all want me when there's so much that could go wrong."

"There's always something that could go wrong in any relationship." When he's not being a smart ass, Soren is a pretty deep thinker. "What can you do? Close yourself off from everything?"

"No, but you know what I'm saying. We're all taking a really big risk."

"So we'll have to be careful," Ash reminds her.

She only rolls her eyes. "Sure. We told ourselves that before, too. And then you guys ended up getting in a fistfight on the ice, and there I was, having to pretend I didn't know anything about it. Do you see the kind of position that puts me in? I have to lie all the time. I don't feel good about it."

"There is a simple solution."

Soren waves a hand in my direction. "By all means."

"If we have a problem with each other, we settle it in private. Between ourselves. No more letting stuff spill out in public. I apologize for letting shit get to me."

"Me, too," Ash murmurs. And he should, since he is the one who started the shit that led to our fight. "I let my personal shit get in the way of what mattered, and I ruined everything. I'm sorry, really, I am."

"I know." Harlow offers him a weak smile that doesn't last for long. "But how do I know I can trust you guys to keep your promise?"

"I guess you're just going to have to trust that being with you is better than not being with you," I say with a shrug. The guys nod their agreement. "Now, we know what happens when we can't handle our shit. That alone should be enough to keep us behaving ourselves."

"That's damn right," Ash agrees.

Harlow still doesn't look convinced, and I hate that. I mean, it's not like I expect her to throw her arms around us all at once and pretend none of this ever happened. She's too smart for that. Still, it would be nice if she weren't quite so distrusting. But if she is, that's our fault, too.

"This is what it's all about," Soren murmurs with a shrug. "We can't always predict what's going to happen or how we're going to feel. But we can look at something and say okay, we're not going to do that again. That was a mistake. we can do better. And that's all we're trying to do – I mean, I know that's all I'm trying to do." He looks around like he's searching for support, and my head bobs up and down in agreement. He put it much better than I ever could have.

When all she does is frown and bite her lip, a desperate groan stirs in my chest. I'm not going to lose her again. I can't. I know damn well it's complicated and dangerous, but she matters too much for me to give up. "Hey. I love you."

Her head snaps back and her eyes bulge, and I almost wish I hadn't said it. I mean, that's not exactly the reaction a guy wants to see when he confesses something like that. I'm not going to take it back, even though instinct tells me to run and hide. I won't. I'm going to stand my ground.

"You do?" It's barely a whisper, like she doesn't believe it. How can she not?

"Yes, I do. I love you. I can't live without you." It's as simple as that. "I'm not a poet. Even though you deserve something a lot more eloquent or whatever, all I can do is tell you the truth."

"He's not the only one." Soren's face is an interesting shade of red. "I love you, too. I'm crazy about you."

"And you know I am, too." Ash runs the backs of his fingers over her bare shoulder.

She releases a shuddering sigh that makes my heart stop beating for one painful second. *Please, don't end this. Please.*

"I love you, too." She looks around at all three of us. "Does that sound insane? I feel like it does. But it's true. I do love you, all of you."

There's no way of knowing where we're going to go next.

But that's a good place to start.

37

HARLOW

I can't believe I'm holding my breath like this, waiting with my heart in my throat. This means so much to him. I would hate to see it not go well. No doubt it would get in his head and maybe even set back his progress. Mindset is tricky that way. Many people don't understand that when a hypochondriac complains about being sick, for example, they genuinely feel sick. In their mind, they're not making anything up, even if they're just as healthy as anybody else.

Ash needs to believe in himself if he's going to keep improving. The first step in that is getting back on the ice today and practicing with his team again.

It's clear from the energy around the rink that I'm not the only one who's concerned. Sure, everybody's doing their best to be lighthearted, to act like this is just another practice. Just another day at work. Nothing out of the ordinary at all. But really, they all know what's riding on it just as much as Ash does.

He'll be fine. He has to be. Skating is as natural to him as breathing. He has to do well. There's no other way this can go.

Still, my hands shake a little as I wait along with everybody else for him to step onto the ice. Don't push yourself too hard. I have to settle for begging him in my head, since I'm not going to embarrass him by shouting that in front of everybody. Besides, he knows his limits. I have to trust him.

I notice Ryder looking my way. He gives me a brief and encouraging nod. It brings to mind our last conversation in Ash's bedroom the morning after the party. *We've all got his back. We won't let him hurt himself.* I just hope Ash allows them to do it. That's the problem. What if he decides he doesn't need anybody's help and goes too far?

This is what it means when you love somebody. You never stop worrying about them. At least, that's what I'm battling while pretending not to care as anything more than a part of the team.

He can do this. I know he can do this.

Still, I hold my breath until he's on the ice. The ear-to-ear smile he wears as the team cheers him on brings tears to my eyes. His eyes look a little watery, too, though I know he would never let himself cry in front of the guys. Instead, he holds his hands up to signal for silence. "I just want to say thank you to everybody here. I'm not sure if I could've made it this far without all of you texting and calling and sending cards and gifts and stuff. I'm damn lucky to have all of you in my corner. Thank you."

That earns him another round of applause, and this time I join in. I know it's not easy for him to show vulnerability, so even a speech like that is a huge step. Maybe this experience has changed him beyond the physical. Maybe he's a little more humble, a little more patient.

"Let's get our asses in gear, because we have a season to save." Yes, that's the Ash I know. I laugh through my tears as the team falls in line for practice drills. He's smiling still, maybe even elated, and my heart is so full I can barely breathe. This is where he belongs. I can't remember the last time I was this happy. This relieved. All of my prayers were answered.

And I wasn't the only one praying. I know that for sure as I look across the rink to where the coaches are gathered. Coach Kozak has his reservations, I'm sure – no matter what Ash wants, it's the coach's job to make sure he's not overdoing it. It's like being a parent, in a way. Just because a kid wants something doesn't mean it's right for them. And it might not be right for Ash to play a full game just yet, or even to go through the rigors of practice along with the team.

But this is a start. I only hope Ash remembers that if the coach asks him to take a step back and rest. Now that he's on the ice, I'm sure he feels invincible. I would hate to see him overdo it because of that.

Still. I can't pretend it isn't sort of thrilling to watch him bounce back the way he has. I'm so proud of how far he's come, and not just in his recovery, either. He's come a long way as a person, too. The chip that was on his shoulder is gone now, and while I'm not naïve enough to think it will never come back, at least he's managed it for now. He can be happy. He can feel good about himself. That's all I want for him, for any of them.

Once practice is over, I hang around for a little while and chat with a few of the players before they head in to take a shower. Part of it is a matter of doing my job, but mostly I'm waiting around for my guys. We made plans to celebrate tonight after Ash's return, so

they'll all be headed back to my house for dinner…
and whatever comes after that. The idea makes my
blood sing in my veins as I climb the steps and leave
the rink, humming happily on my way to my office
to grab my purse. I can't remember the last time I
felt this happy and whole. Everything is the way it
needs to be – it's complicated, sure, but I can't ignore
how it feels to be with them. Everything was off
while we were apart, clunky and awkward and
wrong. There is a sense now of a train returning to
the right track. Like my life is back on course, even
if there are still secrets to keep.

But Soren was right. Now we know what to avoid.
We can keep ourselves safe.

That's what I'm thinking as I open my office door
and step into the darkened room.

Where somebody's waiting for me.

I jump at the sight of a person seated on the sofa.
"You scared me half to death!" I gasp, breathless,
touching a hand to my chest once I recognize Coach
Kozak in the light from the hallway. "What are you
doing, sitting here in the dark?"

It's not what he says. Not at first. It's the silence. It
feels like he sits and stares at me forever. And every
second that passes drains a little more of the air from
the room until I can barely take a breath.

Finally, he takes one. "What have you done?"

"Ex-excuse me?" I stammer.

"You heard me. What have you done? Why? Don't you know how inappropriate it is?"

Oh, no. No, he can't. There's no way.

I can tell myself that all I want, but there's no arguing with the flat disappointment in his eyes.

This is it.

This was my greatest fear.

"I know about you and the players. I know about you and Ryder and Soren and Ash. You are their doctor, Harlow." He's equal parts sad and angry, staring holes through me. "I can't believe you would do something like this."

THANK you for reading Puck Me! Can't wait to find out what happens next? **1-Click Puck It Now!**

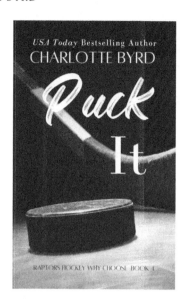

I found love with Ash, Soren and Ryder, three professional hockey players, at the same time. We never expected it to be this way.

There isn't just one person for me. There are three.

Casual surfer dude. Distant Swedish playboy. Broken foster kid.

All arrogant a$$holes on the outside and kind and loving on the inside.

But it's all crashing down.

I'm their team's psychologist and this is beyond inappropriate.

To save our careers, we needed to stop before it was too late.

Now everyone knows and nothing is the same.

But things are about to get even more complicated.

I'm pregnant…

1-Click Puck It Now!

ALSO, if you never read the prequel, One Pucking Night, check it out here and see how Harlow first got into this sticky situation.

1-Click One Pucking Night now!

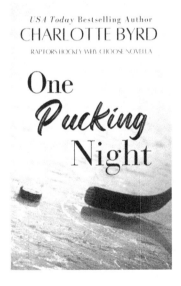

Please take a moment to leave a review on Amazon! Reviews help me find new readers and they can be as short as a sentence. Thank you!

ABOUT CHARLOTTE BYRD

Charlotte Byrd is the bestselling author of romantic suspense novels. She has sold over 1.5 Million books and has been translated into five languages.

She lives near Palm Springs, California with her husband, son, a toy Australian Shepherd and a Ragdoll cat. Charlotte is addicted to books and Netflix and she loves hot weather and crystal blue water.

Write her here:

charlotte@charlotte-byrd.com

Check out her books here:

www.charlotte-byrd.com

Connect with her here:

www.tiktok.com/charlottebyrdbooks

www.facebook.com/charlottebyrdbooks

www.instagram.com/charlottebyrdbooks

Sign up for my newsletter: https://www.
subscribepage.com/byrdVIPList

Join my Facebook Group: https://www.facebook.
com/groups/276340079439433/

Bonus Points: Follow me on BookBub and
Goodreads!

amazon.com/Charlotte-Byrd/e/B013MN45Q6

facebook.com/charlottebyrdbooks

tiktok.com/charlottebyrdbooks

bookbub.com/profile/charlotte-byrd

instagram.com/charlottebyrdbooks

x.com/byrdauthor

ALSO BY CHARLOTTE BYRD

All books are available at ALL major retailers! If you can't find it, please email me at charlotte@ charlotte-byrd.com

Somerset Harbor
Hate Mate (Cargill Brothers 1)
Best Laid Plans (Cargill Brothers 2)
Picture Perfect (Cargill Brothers 3)
Always Never (Cargill Brothers 4)
Kiss Me Again (Macmillan Brothers 1)
Say You'll Stay (Macmillan Brothers 2)
Never Let Go (Macmillan Brothers 3)
Keep Me Close (Macmillan Brothers 4)

Hockey Why Choose
One Pucking Night (Novella)
Kiss and Puck

Pucking Disaster

Puck Me

Puck It

Tell me Series

Tell Me to Stop

Tell Me to Go

Tell Me to Stay

Tell Me to Run

Tell Me to Fight

Tell Me to Lie

Tell Me to Stop Box Set Books 1-6

Black Series

Black Edge

Black Rules

Black Bounds

Black Contract

Black Limit

Black Edge Box Set Books 1-5

Dark Intentions Series

Dark Intentions

Dark Redemption

Dark Sins

Dark Temptations

Dark Inheritance

Dark Intentions Box Set Books 1-5

Tangled Series
Tangled up in Ice
Tangled up in Pain
Tangled up in Lace
Tangled up in Hate
Tangled up in Love

Tangled up in Ice Box Set Books 1-5

The Perfect Stranger Series
The Perfect Stranger
The Perfect Cover
The Perfect Lie
The Perfect Life
The Perfect Getaway

The Perfect Stranger Box Set Books 1-5

Wedlocked Trilogy
Dangerous Engagement
Lethal Wedding
Fatal Wedding

Dangerous Engagement Box Set Books 1-3

Lavish Trilogy
Lavish Lies

Lavish Betrayal

Lavish Obsession

Lavish Lies Box Set Books 1-3

All the Lies Series

All the Lies

All the Secrets

All the Doubts

All the Lies Box Set Books 1-3

Not into you Duet

Not into you

Still not into you

Standalone Novels

Dressing Mr. Dalton

Debt

Offer

Unknown

Made in the USA
Las Vegas, NV
22 December 2023

83457423R00184